William Hayley

The Triumphs of Temper

A Poem, in Six Cantos. Sixth Edition

William Hayley

The Triumphs of Temper
A Poem, in Six Cantos. Sixth Edition

ISBN/EAN: 9783744716253

Printed in Europe, USA, Canada, Australia, Japan

Cover: Foto ©Andreas Hilbeck / pixelio.de

More available books at **www.hansebooks.com**

THE
TRIUMPHS OF TEMPER;

A

P O E M:

IN SIX CANTOS.

BY

WILLIAM HAYLEY, Esq.

O voi ch' avete gl' intelletti fani
Mirate la dottrina, che fi afconde
Sotto' il velame degli verfi ftrani.

DANTE, Inferno, Canto 9.

THE SIXTH EDITION, CORRECTED.

LONDON:

PRINTED FOR T. CADELL, IN THE STRAND.

M.DCC.LXXXVIII.

P R E F A C E.

*I*T *ſeems to be a kind of duty incumbent on thoſe*
who devote themſelves to poetry, to raiſe, if poſſible,
the dignity of a declining art, by making it as bene-
ficial to life and manners as the limits of compoſition,
and the character of modern times, will allow. The
ages, indeed, are paſt, in which the ſong of the poet
was idolized for its miraculous effects; *yet a poem,*
intended to promote the cultivation of good-humour,
may ſtill perhaps be fortunate enough to prove of
ſome little ſervice to ſociety in general; or, if this
idea may be thought too chimerical and romantic
by ſober reaſon, it is at leaſt one of thoſe pleaſing
and innocent deluſions, in which a poetical enthu-
ſiaſt may be ſafely indulged.

A 3

The

The following production owes its existence to an incident in real life, very similar to the principal action of the last canto; but in forming the general plan of the work, it seemed to me absolutely necessary to introduce both the agency and the abode of SPLEEN, *notwithstanding the difficulty and the hazard of attempting a subject so happily executed by the masterly pencil of Pope. I considered his Cave of Spleen as a most exquisite cabinet picture; and, to avoid the servility of imitation, I determined to sketch the mansion of this gloomy power on a much wider canvass: happy, indeed, if the judgment of the public may enable me to exclaim, with the honest vanity of the painter, who compared his own works to the divine productions of Raphael,*

" E son pittore anch' Io !"

The celebrated Alessandro Tassoni, who is generally considered as the inventor of the modern Heroi-comic

comic poetry, was so proud of having extended the limits of his art by a new kind of composition, that he not only spoke of it with infinite exultation in one of his private letters, but even gave a MS. copy of his work to his native city of Modena, with an inscription, in which he stiled it a new species of poetry, invented by himself.

A few partial friends have asserted, that the present performance has some degree of similar merit; but as I apprehend all the novelty it possesses, may rather require an apology, than entitle its author to challenge commendation, I shall explain how far the conduct of the poem differs from the most approved models in this mode of writing, and slightly mention the poetical effects, which such a variation appeared likely to produce.

It is well known, that the favourite poems, which blend the serious and the comic, represent

A 4   their

their principal characters in a satirical point of view: it was the intention of Tassoni (though prudence made him attempt to conceal it) to satirize a particular Italian nobleman, who happened to be the object of his resentment. Boileau *openly ridicules the French ecclesiastics in his* Lutrin*;* Garth*, our English physicians, in his* Dispensary*; and the* Rape of the Lock *itself, that most excellent and enchanting poem, which I never contemplate but with new idolatry, is denominated* the best satire extant, *by the learned Dr.* Warton*, in his very elegant and ingenious, but severe,* Essay on Pope*: a sentence which seems to be confirmed by the poet himself, in his letter to Mrs.* Fermor*, where he says, " the character of* Belinda*, as it is now managed, resembles you in nothing but in beauty." Though I think, that no composition can surpass, or perhaps ever equal this most happy effort of genius, as a sportive satire, I imagined it might be possible to give a new character to this mixed species*

of

of poetry, and to render it by its object, though not in its execution, more noble than the most beautiful and refined satire can be. We have seen it carried to inimitable perfection, in the most delicate raillery on female foibles: —— it remained to be tried, if it might not also aspire to delineate the more engaging features of female excellence. The idea appeared to me worth the experiment; for, if it succeeded, it seemed to promise a double advantage; first, it would give an air of novelty to the poem; and, secondly, what I thought of much greater importance, it would render it more interesting to the heart. On these principles, I have endeavoured to paint SERENA *as a most lovely, engaging, and accomplished character; yet I hope the colouring is so faithfully copied from* general nature, *that every man, who reads the poem, may be happy enough to know many fair ones, who resemble my heroine.*

There

There is another point, in which I have also attempted to give this poem an air of novelty: I mean, the manner of connecting the real and the visionary scenes, which compose it; by shifting these in alternate cantos, I hoped to make familiar incident and allegorical picture afford a strong relief to each other, and keep the attention of the reader alive, by an appearance particularly diversified. I wished, indeed (but I fear most ineffectually) for powers to unite some touches of the sportive wildness of Ariosto, and the more serious sublime painting of Dante, with some portion of the enchanting elegance, the refined imagination, and the moral graces of Pope; and to do this, if possible, without violating those rules of propriety, which Mr. Cambridge has illustrated, by example as well as precept, in the Scribleriad, and in his sensible preface to that elegant and learned poem.

I have

I have now very frankly informed my reader of the extent, *or rather the* extravagance *of my desire; for I will not give it the serious name of* design : *They, whom an enlightened taste has rendered thoroughly sensible how very difficult it must be to accomplish such an idea, will not only be the first to discern, but the most ready to pardon those errors, into which so hazardous an attempt may perhaps have betrayed me. I had thoughts of introducing this performance to the public, by a dissertation of considerable length on this species of poetry; but I forbear to indulge myself any farther in such preliminary remarks, as the anxiety of authors is so apt to produce, from the reflection, that, however ingeniously written, they add little or nothing to the success of a good poem, and are utterly insufficient to prevent that neglect, or oblivion, which is the inevitable fate of a bad one.*

In

In dismissing a work to my fair readers, which is intended principally for their perusal, I shall only recommend it to their attention; and bid them farewell, in the words of the pleasant and courteous Tassoni—

" *Vaglia il buon voler, s' altro non lice,*
    E chi la leggera, viva felice! "

EARTHAM,
    Jan. 31, 1781.

                                    T H E

TRIUMPHS OF TEMPER.

CANTO I.

THE mind's foft guardian, who, tho' yet unfung,
Infpires with harmony the female tongue,
And gives, improving every tender grace,
The fmile of angels to a mortal face;
Her powers I fing; and fcenes of mental ftrife,
Which form the maiden for th' accomplifh'd wife;
Where the fweet victor fees, with fparkling eyes,
Love her reward, and happinefs her prize.
Daughters of beauty, who the fong infpire,
To your enchanting notes attune my lyre!
And O! if haply your foft hearts may gain
Or ufe, or pleafure from the motley ftrain,

B

Tho'

Tho' formal critics, with a furly frown,

Deny your artlefs bard the laurel crown,

He ftill fhall triumph, if ye deign to fpread

Your fweeter myrtle round his honour'd head.

    In your bright circle young SERENA grew;

· A lovelier nymph the pencil never drew;

For the fond Graces form'd her eafy mien,

And heaven's foft azure in her eye was feen.

She feem'd a rofe-bud, when it firft receives

The genial fun in its expanding leaves:

For now fhe enter'd thofe important years,

When the full bofom fwells with hopes and fears;

When confcious nature prompts the fecret figh,

And fheds fweet languor o'er the melting eye;

When nobler toys the female heart trepan,

And dolls rejected, yield their place to man.

    Beneath a father's care SERENA grew;

The good SIR GILBERT, to his country true,

A faithful Whig, who, zealous for the ftate,

In freedom's fervice led the loud debate;

                        Yet

Yet every day, by tranſmutation rare,
Turn'd to a Tory in his elbow-chair,
And made his daughter pay, howe'er abſurd,
Paſſive obedience to his ſovereign word.

   In his domeſtic ſway he borrow'd aid
From prim PENELOPE, an ancient maid,
His upright ſiſter, conſcious of her worth,
Who valued ſtill her beauty, and her birth ;
Tho' from her birth no envied rank ſhe gain'd,.
And of her beauty but the ghoſt remain'd ;
A reſtleſs ghoſt ! that with remembrance keen
Proclaim'd inceſſant what it once had been ;
Delighted ſtill the ſteps of youth to haunt,
To watch the tender nymph, and warm gallant ;
And, with an eye that petrified purſuit,
Hang like the dragon o'er th' Heſperian fruit.

   Tho' ſtrictly guarded by this jealous power,
The mild SERENA no reſtraint could four :
Pure was her boſom, as the ſilver lake,
Ere riſing winds the ruffled water ſhake,

           When

When the bright pageants of the morning fky,

Acrofs th' expanfive mirror lightly fly,

By vernal gales in quick fucceffion driven,

While the clear glafs reflects the fmile of heaven.

In gay content a fportive life fhe led,

The child of Modefty, by Virtue bred :

Her light companions Innocence and Eafe :

Her hope was pleafure, and her wifh to pleafe :

For this, to Fafhion early rites fhe paid ;

For this, to Venus fecret vows fhe made ;

Nor held it fin to caft a private glance

O'er the dear pages of a new romance,

Eager in fiction's touching fcenes to find

A field, to exercife her youthful mind :

The touching fcenes new energy impreft

On all the virtues of her feeling breaft.

Sweet Evelina's fafcinating power

Had firft beguil'd of fleep her midnight hour :

Poffeft by fympathy's enchanting fway,

She read, unconfcious of the dawning day.

The

Stothard del.   Sharp sculp.

London, Publish'd Sept.r 1.st 1787, by T. Cadell, Strand.

The Modern Anecdote was next convey'd
Beneath her pillow by her faithful maid.
The nymph, attentive as the brooding dove,
Por'd o'er the tender scenes of Franzel's love :
. The sinking taper now grew weak and pale ;
Serena sigh'd, and dropt th' unfinish'd tale ;
But, as warm clouds in vernal æther roll,
The soft ideas floated in her soul :
Free from ambitious pride, and envious care,
To love, and to be lov'd, was all her prayer :
While these fond thoughts her gentle mind possess'd,
Soft slumber settled on her snowy breast.

Scarce had her radiant eyes began to close,
When to her view a friendly vision rose :
A fairy Phantom struck her mental sight,
. Light as the gossamer, as æther bright ;
Array'd like Pallas was the pigmy form,
When the sage Goddess stills the martial storm.
Her casque was amber, richly grac'd above
With down, collected from the callow dove :

Her

Her burniſh'd breaſt-plate, of a deeper dye,

Was once the armour of a golden fly :

A lynx's eye her little ægis ſhone,

By fairy ſpells converted into ſtone,

And worn of old, as elfin poets ſing,

By Ægypt's lovely queen, a favourite ring :

Myſterious power was in the magic toy,

To turn the frowns of care to ſmiles of joy.

Her tiny lance, whoſe radiance ſtream'd afar,

Was one bright ſparkle from the bridal ſtar.

A filmy mantle round her figure play'd,

Fine as the texture, by Arachne laid

O'er ſome young plant, when glittering to the view

With many an orient pearl of morning dew.

The Phantom hover'd o'er the conſcious Fair

With ſuch a lively ſmile of tender care,

As on her elfin lord Titania caſt,

When firſt ſhe found his angry ſpell was paſt.

Round her rich locks S E R E N A chanc'd to tie

. An ample ribband of cærulean dye :

High

High o'er her forehead rofe the graceful bow,
Whofe arch commanded the fweet fcene below :
The hovering Spirit view'd the tempting fpot,
And lightly perch'd on this unbending knot ;
As the fair flutterer, of Pfyche's race,
Is feen to terminate her airy chace,
When, pleas'd at length her quivering wings to clofe,
Fondly fhe fettles on the fragrant rofe.

   Now in foft notes, more mufically clear
Than ever Fairy breath'd in mortal ear,
Thefe words the vifionary voice convey'd
To the charm'd fpirit of the fleeping maid :

   " Thou darling of my care, whofe ripen'd worth
Shall fpread my empire o'er the fmiling earth ;
Whom Nature bleft, forbidding modifh Art
To cramp thy fpirit, or contract thy heart ;
Screen'd from thy thought, nor in thy vifions felt,
Long on thy opening mind I've fondly dwelt ;
In childhood's forrows brought thee quick relief,
And dry'd thy April fhowers of infant grief:

Taught

Taught thee to laugh at the malicious boy,

Who broke thy playthings with a barbarous joy,

. To bear what ills the little female haunt,

The tefty nurfe, th' imperious governante,

. And that tyrannic peft, the prying maiden aunt.

Now ripening years a nobler fcene fupply ;

For life now opens on thy fparkling eye :

Thy rifing bofom fwells with juft defire

Rapture to feel, and rapture to infpire :

Not the vain blifs, the tranfitory joys,

That childifh woman feels, in radiant toys ;

The coftly diamond, or the lighter pearl,

The maffive Nabob, or the tinfel Earl.

Thy heart demands, each meaner aim above,

. Th' imperifhable wealth of fterling love ;

Thy wifh, to pleafe by ev'ry fofter grace

Of elegance and eafe, of form and face !

. By lively fancy and by fenfe refin'd,

The ftronger magic of the cultur'd mind !

Thy pure ambition, and thy virtuous plan,

. To fix the variable heart of man !

Short

Short is the worſhip paid at beauty's ſhrine;

But laſting love and happineſs are mine:

Mine, tho' the earth's miſtaken, blinded race

Deſpiſe my influence, and my name debaſe;

Nor breathe one vow to that ætherial friend,

On whom the colours of their life depend.

But to thy innocence I now diſplay

The myſtic marvels of my ſecret ſway;

And tell, in this thy fate-deciding hour,

My race, my name, my office, and my power.

　　Firſt, hear what wonders human forms contain!

And learn the texture of the female brain!

By Nature's care in curious order ſpread,

This living net is fram'd of tender thread;

Fine, as thy hand, ſome favour'd youth to grace,

Knits with nice art to form the mimic lace.

Within the center of this fretted dome,

Her ſecret tower, her heaven-conſtructed home,

. Soft Senſibility, ſweet Beauty's ſoul!

Keeps her coy ſtate, and animates the whole,

Inviſible

Invifible as Harmony, who fprings,

Wak'd by young Zephyr, from Æolian ftrings :

Her fubtle power, more delicately fine,

Dwells in each thread, and lives in every line,

Whofe quick vibrations, without end, impart

Pleafure and pain to the refponfive heart.

As Zephyr's breath the willing chord infpires,

Whifpering foft mufic to the trembling wires,

So with fond care I regulate, unfeen,

The fofter movements of this nice machine ;

TEMPER my earthly name, the nurfe of Love !

But call'd SOPHROSYNE in realms above !

When lovely Woman, perfeſt at her birth,

Bleft with her early charms the wond'ring earth,

Her foul, in fweet fimplicity array'd,

Nor fhar'd my guidance, nor requir'd my aid.

Her tender frame, nor confident nor coy,

Had every fibre tun'd to gentle joy :

No vain caprices fwell'd her pouting lip ;

No gold produc'd a mercenary trip ;

Soft

Soft innocence infpir'd her willing kifs,
. Her love was nature, and her life was blifs.
Guide of his reafon, not his paffion's prey,
She tam'd the favage, Man, who blefs'd her fway.
No jarring wifhes fill'd the world with woes,
But youth was ecftacy, and age repofe.
    The Powers of Mifchief met, in dark Divan,
To blaft thefe mighty joys of envied Man :
The Fiends, at their infernal leader's call,
Fram'd their bafe wiles in Demogorgon's hall.
In the deep center of that dreadful dome,
An hellifh cauldron boil'd with fiery foam :
In this wide urn the circling fpirits threw
Ingredients harfh, and hideous to the view.;
While the terrific mafter of the fpell
With adjurations fhook the depths of hell,
And in dark words, unmeet for mortal ear,
Bade the dire offspring of his art appear.
Forth from the vafe, with fullen murmurs, broke
A towering mafs of peftilential fmoke :

                                    Emerging

Emerging from this fog of thickeſt night,
A Phantom ſwells, by ſlow degrees, to ſight ;
But ere the view can ſeize the forming ſhape,
From the mock'd eye its lineaments eſcape :
. It ſeem'd all paſſions melted into one,
Aſſum'd the face of all, and yet was none :
Hell ſtood aghaſt at its portentous mien,
And ſhuddering Demons call'd the ſpeſtre Spleen.
' Hie thee to earth !' its mighty maſter cried,
' O'er the vex'd globe in heavy vapours ride !
Within its center fix thy ſhadowy throne !
With ſhades thy ſubjeſts, and that hell thy own !
Reign there unſeen ! but let thy ſtrong controul
Be hourly felt in Woman's wayward ſoul !
With darkeſt poiſons from our deep abyſs,
Taint that pure fountain of terreſtrial bliſs !'
Th' enormous Phantom, at this potent ſound,
Roll'd forth obedient from the vaſt profound :
The quaking Fiends recover'd from their dread,
And hell grew lighter, as the monſter fled.
                                        But

Stothard del.   Sharp sculp.

London Publijhed Sepr.r.1781. by T. Cadell Strand

But now round earth the gliding vapours run,

Blot the rich æther, and eclipfe the fun ;

All Nature fickens ; and her faireft flower,

Enchanting Woman, feels the baneful Power :

As in her foul the clouds of Spleen arife,

The fprightly effence of her beauty flies :

In youth's gay prime, in hours with rapture warm,

Love looks aftonifh'd on her altering form :

To pleafing frolics, and enchanting wiles,

Life-darting looks, and foul-fubduing fmiles,

Dark whims fucceed : thick-coming fancies fret ;

The fullen paffion, and the hafty pet ;

The fwelling lip, the tear-diftended eye,

The peevifh queftion, the perverfe reply ;

The moody humour, that, like rain and fire,

Blends cold difguft with unfubdu'd defire,

Flies what it loves, and, petulantly coy,

Feigns proud abhorrence of the proffer'd joy :

For Nature's artlefs aim, the wifh to pleafe

By genuine modefty, and fimple eafe,

Fafhion's

Fashion's pert tricks the crowded brain oppress

. With all the poor parade of tawdry dress :

The sickly bosom pants for noise and show,

For every bauble, and for every beau ;

The voice, that health made harmony, disowns

That native charm for languor's mimic tones ;

And feigns disease, till, feeling what it feigns,

Its fancied maladies are real pains.

Such, and a thousand still superior woes,

From Spleen's new empire o'er the earth arose :

Each simple dictate of the soul forgot,

Then first was form'd the mercenary plot ;

And beauty practis'd that pernicious art,

The art of angling for an old man's heart ;

Tho' crawling to his bride with tottering knees,

His words were dotage, and his love disease.

From sex to sex this base contagion ran,

And gold grew beauty in the eyes of man :

Courtship was traffic : and the married life

. But one loud jangle of incessant strife.

The

The gentle Sprite, who, on his radiant car,
, Shines the mild regent of the evening-ftar,
And joys from thence thofe genial rays to fhed,
That lead the bridegroom to the nuptial bed,
While earth's new ills his friendly foul abforb,
From Cynthia call'd me to his kindred orb;
And, eager to redrefs the woes of man,
The brilliant Son of Vefper thus began:
' Thou fofteft Being of th' ætherial kind,
Be thy benignant cares no more confin'd
To fmooth the ruffled plume of Zephyr's wing,
To guard from cruel froft the infant fpring,
To drive grofs atoms from the rays of noon,
Or chafe the halo from the vapourifh moon!
Thy friendly nature will not now deny
To quit for nobler toils thy native fky;
Thou feeft how Spleen's infernal vapours roll
. Acrofs the fweet ferene of woman's foul;
And earth, which darkens as her beauties fade,
Muft grow a fecond hell without thy aid:

Take

Take then thy ftation! fix thy nobler reign
O'er thofe fine chords, that form the female brain,
That us'd, ere injur'd by the ruft of Spleen,
To fill with harmony the human fcene!
Go! left her touch their tender tones deftroy,
Teach them to vibrate to thy notes of joy!
Go! and reftore, by ftilling mental ftrife,
Health to faint love, and happinefs to life!'
So fpake that friend of man, who lights above
His heavenly lamp of Hymenæal love:
In his juft aim my kindred fpirit join'd,
And flew obedient to the charge affign'd.
Hence, as the bias fways th' unconfcious bowl,
I long unfeen have fway'd the carelefs foul;
Tho' oft I feel my power by Spleen fubdu'd,
In the fhrill vixen, and the fullen prude,
In fome fair forms my foft dominion grows,
Like fragrance, rifing from the opening rofe:
Still I preferve, in many a lovely face,
.That gay good-humour, and that conftant grace,

Which

Which heavenly Powers united to infold

In perfect Woman's new-created mould;

When Nature, in her infant beauty bleft,

The laft and lovelieft of her works careft.

But of thofe nymphs, who, delicately fair,

Draw their foft graces from my forming care,

My young SERENA fhines her peers above,

Pride of my hopes, and darling of my love.

Hence I to thee fuch myfteries unfold,

As Man's pedantic eye fhall ne'er behold;

Whofe narrow fcience, tho' it proudly boaft

To pierce the fky, and count the ftarry hoft,

Sees not the lucid band of airy Powers,

Who flutter round him in his fecret hours:

But if to me, thy guardian now difplay'd,

Thy duteous orifons are juftly paid,

Thou to thofe realms fhalt pafs with me thy guide,

Where Spleen's pale victims, after death, refide;

Then to that orb, in vifion fhalt thou rife,

Unfeen by mortal aftronomic eyes,

C

Where

Where I—but first let me thy soul prepare

To meet our secret foe's insidious snare!

'Tis my fond purpose in thy form to show

. The sweetest model of my skill below :

A youth I destine to thy dear embrace,

Crown'd with each mental charm, and manly grace,

With whom thy innocence, secure from strife,

Shall reap the beauteous joys of blameless life.

Pleas'd I observe thy little heart begin

To ask, what charms the mighty prize may win :

But know, tho' Elegance herself be seen

To guide thy motion, and to form thy mien ;

Tho' Beauty o'er thy filial cheek diffuse

The soft enchantment of her roseate hues,

Not from their favour shall this glory rise !

. TEMPER shall singly gain the splendid prize :

The sudden conquest shall be mine alone,

And Love with transport shall my triumph own.

Such are my hopes ; but I with pain relate

What hard conditions are annex'd by fate :

As

As chemic fires, that patient labour blows,
Draw the rich perfume from the Perſian roſe,
So muſt thou form, by fiery toils refin'd,
The living eſſence of thy ſweeter mind.
Dimly I ſee, on Deſtiny's dull glaſs,
Three dangerous trials 'tis thy doom to paſs ;
And oh ! if once forgetful of my power,
Good-humour fail thee in the fateful hour,
Farewell thoſe joys, that wait the happy wife !
Farewell the viſion of unclouded life !

Fain would my love thy ſecret perils ſhow,
Which fate allows not even me to know :
In Spleen's dark court a thouſand agents dwell,
Who bind her victims in the wayward ſpell ;
Perchance three prime ſupporters of her ſway,
The buſieſt of her fiends, may croſs thy way :
Stern Contradiction, her ill-favour'd child,
Of fierce demeanor, and of ſpirit wild,
Bane of delight ! and horror of the ſex !
His plan to puzzle, and his pride to vex !—

Or Scandal, filthy hag ! who blindly limps
Round the wide earth, fupported by her imps,
Her inky demons, who delight to print
Her bafe fuggeftion, and her envious hint :—
. Or groundlefs Jealoufy, pert changeling ! born
Of amprous Vanity, and angry Scorn,
Whofe bitter taunts with public infult dare
Bafely to wound the unoffending fair,
Proud the fweet joys of innocence to crufh,
And fpread o'er beauty's cheek the burning blufh.
Whether thefe kindred fiends, or one or all,
Shall aim thy airy fpirit to enthrall,
Are points, my fondnefs tries in vain to reach ;
But truft my caution ! and beware of each !

Left to thy lively mind my words may feem
The vain chimera of a common dream,
By one unqueftionable fign be taught
To prize my prefence in thy waking thought !
An azure ribband, on thy toilet thrown,
Shall make the magic of my empire known :

On

On this thy fportive needle tried its powers,

And filver fpangles form'd the mimic flowers ;

On thefe my love fhall breathe a fecret charm ;

With this, my cæftus, thy foft bofom arm !

Above it let the decent tucker rife,

To hide the myftic band from mortal eyes !

When Spleen's dark Powers would teach that breaft

    to fwell,

This guardian cincture fhall thofe Powers repel :

. As the touch'd talifman, more fwift than thought,

To fave'her charge, th' Arabian Fairy brought ;

So fhall this zone, if juftly I'm obey'd,

Bring my foft fpirit to thy certain aid.

. In Love's great name obferve this high beheft !

Revere my power—Be gentle, and be bleft !"

    Here the kind Sprite her friendly counfel clos'd,

And lightly vanifh'd—Still SERENA doz'd ;

Still in fweet trance fhe fondly feem'd to hear

The foft perfuafion vibrate in her ear.

But waking now far different notes fhe found ;

Lefs pleafing echoes in her chamber found :

. For now the heralds of the London day
Sing their loud mattins in th' uncrowded way ;
Th' impatient milk-maid now, with early din,
Screams to the rattle of her pail of tin ;
With fweep's faint cry, and, lateft of the crew,
The deep-ton'd mufic of the murmuring Jew.

END OF THE FIRST CANTO.

CANTO

C A N T O   II.

YE radiant nymphs ! whofe opening eyes convey
Warmth to the world, and luftre to the day !
Think what o'erfhadowing clouds may crofs your
    brain,
Before thofe lovely lids fhall clofe again !
What funds of patience twelve long hours may afk,
When cold Difcretion claims her daily tafk !
Ah think betimes ! and, while your morning care
Sheds foreign odors o'er your fragrant hair,
Tinge your foft fpirit with that mental fweet,
Which may not be exhal'd by paffion's heat ;
But charm the fenfe, with undecaying power,
Thro' every chance of each diurnal hour !
O ! might you all perceive your toilets crown'd
With fuch cofmetics as SERENA found !
For, to the warning vifion fondly true,
Now the quick fair-one to the toilet flew :

     With

With keen delight her ravifh'd eye furvey'd
The myftic ribband on her mirror laid:
Bright fhone the azure as Aurora's car,
And every fpangle feem'd a living ftar.
With fportive grace the fmiling damfel preft
The guardian cincture to her fnowy breaft,
More lovely far than Juno, when fhe ftrove
To look moft lovely in the eyes of Jove;
And willing Venus lent her every power,
That fheds enchantment o'er the amorous hour:
For fpells more potent on this band were thrown,
Than Venus boafted in her beauteous zone.
Her dazzling cæftus could alone infpire
The fudden impulfe of fhort-liv'd defire:
Thefe finer threads with lafting charms are fraught,
Here lies the tender, but unchanging thought,
Silence, that wins, where eloquence is vain,
And tones, that harmonize the mad'ning brain,
Soft fighs, that anger cannot hear, and live,
And fmiles, that tell, how truly they forgive.;

And

And lively grace, whofe gay diffufive light
Puts the black phantoms of the brain to flight,
Whofe cheering powers thro' every period laft,
And make the prefent happy as the paft.

   Such fecret charms this richer zone poffeft,
Whofe flowers, now fparkling on SERENA's breaft,
Give, tho' unfeen thofe fwelling orbs they bind,
Smiles to her face, and beauty to her mind:
For now, obfervant of the Sprite's beheft,
The nymph conceals them by her upper veft:
Safe lies the fpell, no mortal may defcry,
Not keen PENELOPE's all-piercing eye;
Who conftant, as the fteps of morn advance,
Surveys the houfhold with a fearching glance,
And entering now, with all her ufual care,
Reviews the chamber of the youthful fair.
Beneath the pillow, not compleatly hid,
The novel lay—She faw—fhe feiz'd—fhe chid:
With rage and glee her glaring eye-balls flafh,
Ah wicked age! fhe cries, ah filthy trafh!

From

From the firſt page my juſt abhorrence ſprings ;

For modern anecdotes are monſtrous things :

Yet will I ſee what dangerous poiſons lurk,

To taint thy youth, in this licentious work.

She ſaid : and rudely from the chamber ruſh'd,

Her pallid cheek with expeƈtation fluſh'd,

With ardent hope her eager ſpirit ſhook,

Vain hope ! to banquet on a luſcious book.

So if a prieſt, of the Arabian ſeƈt,

In Turkiſh hands forbidden wine deteƈt,

The ſacred muſſulman, with pious din,

Arraigns the culprit, and proclaims the ſin,

Curſes with holy zeal th' inflaming juice,

But curſing takes it for his ſecret uſe.

  The gay SERENA, with unruffled mind,

The pleaſing novel, thus unread, reſign'd.

The viſion on her ſoul ſuch virtue left,

She only ſmil'd at the provoking theft ;

The teazing incident ſhe deem'd a jeſt,

Nor felt the zone grow tighter on her breaſt.

                                        Now

Now in full charms defcends the finifh'd fair,

For now the morning banquet claims her care ;

Already at the board, with viands pil'd,

Her fire impatient fits, and chides his tardy child.

On his imperial lips rude hunger reigns,

And keener politics ufurp his brains :

But when her love-infpiring voice he hears,

When the foft magic of her fmile appears,

In that glad moment he at once forgets

His empty ftomach, and the nation's debts :

He bends to Nature's more divine controul,

And only feels the Father in his foul.

Quick to his hand behold her now prefent

The Indian liquor of celeftial fcent !

Not with more grace the nectar'd cup is given

By rofe-lip'd Hebe to the lord of heaven.

While her fair hands a frefh libation pour,

Fafhion's loud thunder wakes the founding door.

The light SERENA to the window fprings,

On curiofity's amufive wings :

Her quick eyes fparkle with furprife, to fee
The glories of a golden vis-à-vis :
Its glittering tablet gleam'd with mimic pearl,
And the rich coronet announc'd an earl.
The good old knight grew fomewhat proud to hear
Of this new vifit from the early peer :
SERENA recollects the vifion's truth,
And fluttering, hopes it is the promis'd youth :
PENELOPE from her high chamber peeps ;
There her unfinifh'd charms fhe coyly keeps ;
With fage referve her modefty abhorr'd
To fhew her morning face before a lord.

    The peer alights : the well-rang'd vaffals bawl
His founding title thro' the fpacious hall,
Till in the deep faloon's extremeft bound
Th' ear-tickling words, " LORD FILLIGREE,"
    refound.
As when great Hector, fetting war apart,
Advanc'd to parley, with his fpear athwart,
The Greeks beheld him with a ftill delight ;
And filent reverence ftopt the rifing fight ;

With

With fuch refpect, but unchaftis'd by fear,

SIR GILBERT and the nymph firft meet the peer;

And, while his morning compliments commence,

The flighted breakfaft ftands in cold fufpence.

But far unlike to Hector's ruder grace

His modern ftature, and his modifh face!

Nor lefs he differs from thofe barons old,

Whofe arms are blazon'd on his car of gold;

Whofe proftrate caftle guarded once the lands,

Where, fpruce in motley pride, his villa ftands,

By Tafte erected, in her trimmeft mode,

Her mufhroom ftructure, and her quaint abode.

As the neat daify to the fun's broad flower,

As the French boudoir to the Gothic tower,

Such is the peer, whom fafhion much admires,

Compar'd in perfon to his ancient fires:

For their broad fhoulder, and their brawny calf,

Their coarfe, loud language, and their coarfer laugh,

His finer form, more elegantly flim,

Difplays the fafhionable length of limb:

With

With foreign fhrugs his country he regards,

And her lean tongue with foreign words he lards ;

While Gallic Graces, who correƈ his ftyle,

Forbid his mirth to pafs beyond a fmile.

As the nice workman in the wooden trade,

Hides his coarfe ground, with fineft woods o'erlaid,

Thus our young lord, with fafhion's phrafe refin'd,

Fineer'd the mean interior of his mind :

And hence, in courtefy's foft luftre feen,

His fpirit fhone, as graceful as his mien.

The artlefs fair, on fafhion's kind report,

Thought him the mirror of a matchlefs court :

Much fhe his drefs, his language much obferves,

Whofe finer accents prove his feeling nerves.

Her fancy now the deftin'd lover fpies,

But her free heart abjures the quick furmife ;

Yet as he fpoke, at every flattering word

The vifion's promife to her thought recurr'd.

Far more parental pride contrives to blind

The good Sir Gilbert's more-experienc'd mind,

Who

Who fondly faw, and at the profpect fmil'd,

A future countefs in his favourite child.

But what new flutterings fhook SERENA's breaft,

What hopes and fears the modeft nymph oppreft,

When with a fimpering fmile, and foft regard,

The peer difplay'd a mirth-expreffive card,

Where the gay Graces, in a fportive band,

Shew the fweet art of Cipriani's hand;

Where, in their train, his airy Cupids throng,

And laughing drag a comic mafk along!

" We," cries my lord, with felf-fufficient joy,

Twirling, with lordly airs, the graceful toy,

" We, who poffefs true fcience, we, who give -

The world a leffon in the art to live,

We for the fair a fplendid fête defign,

And pay our homage thus at Beauty's fhrine."

He fpoke; and fpeaking, to the blufhing maid,

With modifh eafe, th' inviting card convey'd,

Where Mirth announc'd her mafque-devoted hour

In characters intwin'd with many a flower:

The

The blushing maid, with eyes of quick desire,

View'd it, and felt her little soul on fire;

For of all scenes she had not yet survey'd,

Her heart most panted for a masquerade:

But her gay hopes increasing terrors drown,

And dread forebodings of her father's frown.

In mute suspence to read his thought she tries,

And strongly pleads with her prevailing eyes,

Her eyes, for doubt enchain'd her modest tongue,

While on his sovereign word her pleasure hung.

With such a tender, and persuasive air

Of soft endearment, and of anxious care,

Thetis attended from th' almighty sire

His fateful answer to her fond desire:

The good old knight, like the Olympian god,

Blest the fair suppliant with his gracious nod;

Her lively spirit the kind signal took,

And her glad heart in every fibre shook.

The party settled, it imports not how,

The peer politely made his parting bow:

The nymph, with eyes that fparkled joyous fire,

Kifs'd the round cheek of her complying fire,

Then fwiftly flew, and fummon'd to her aid

Th' important counfel of her favourite maid,

To vent her joy, and, as the moments prefs,

To fix that firft of points, a fancy-drefs.

Quick as the poet's eyes o'er nature fly,

Piercing the deep, or traverfing the fky,

With fuch light fpeed her fond ideas glance

O'er play and poem, ftory and romance,

While all the characters, fhe e'er has read,

Flafh on her brain, and fill her bufy head.

Now in Diana's form fhe hopes to meet

A fond Endymion fighing at her feet ;

Now her proud thought terreftrial pomp affumes,

. And Dian's crefcent yields to Indian plumes ;

Now, in the habit of the Grecian ifles,

She hears fome Ofman fuing for her fmiles,

And fees his foul that blaze of drefs outfhine,

Whofe wealth impoverifh'd a diamond-mine ;

D   Now

Now fimpler charms her quick attention draw,

The rofe-crown'd bonnet, and the hat of ftraw,

A village-maid fhe feems, in neat attire,

A faithful fhepherd now her fole defire.

Thus, as new figures in her fancy throng,

" She's every thing by ftarts, and nothing long ;"

But, in the fpace of one revolving hour,

Flies thro' all ftates of poverty and power,

All forms, on whom her veering mind can pitch,

Sultana, gipfy, goddefs, nymph, and witch.

At length, her foul with Shakefpeare's magic fraught,

The wand of Ariel fixt her roving thought ;

Ariel's light graces all her heart poffefs,

And Jenny's order'd to prepare the drefs.

It feems already bought, with fond applaufe ;

An azure tiffue, and a filver gauze ;

Too foon, alas ! that garb of heavenly hue

The ready mercer flafhes to her view.

Ah blind to fate ! how oft the youthful belle

Feels her gay heart at fight of tiffue fwell !

                                        And

And thinks the fashionable silk must prove

Her robe of triumph, and a spell to love !

To thee, sweet maid, whose pleasure-darting eyes

Joy in this favourite vest, an hour shall rise,

When thou shalt hate the silk so fondly sought,

And wish thy silver-spotted gauze unbought * :

For busy Spleen thy trial now prepares ;

Darkly she forms her unsuspected snares,

And, keen to raise her pleasure-killing storm,

Assumes PENELOPE's congenial form.

In that prim shape, which all the graces shun,

See the sour fiend to good SIR GILBERT run !

Where, deeply pondering the public debt,

Silent he muses o'er a new gazette !

Ent'ring, she view'd, with eyes of envious spite,

The card, that spoke the masque-devoted night:

---

* Nescia mens hominum fati sortisque futuræ,
  Et servare modum, rebus sublata secundis.
  Turno tempus erit, magno cum optaverit emptum
  Intactum Pallanta, et cum spolia ista diemque
  Oderit.   ÆNEID. x. v. 501. & seq.

Eager

Eager fhe darted on the graceful toy,
And, fiercely pointing to each naked boy,
" Canft thou," fhe cried, in a difcordant fcream,
That rous'd the politician from his dream,
While with her voice the echoing chamber rings,
" * Say! canft thou fuffer thefe flagitious things?
Are thefe devices to thy daughter brought,
That wake fuch grofs impurity of thought?
In vain are all the prudent words I preach,
The modeft maxims that I ftrive to teach;
By foolifh fondnefs of your fenfe beguil'd,
You ftill indulge, and fpoil the flippant child:
For me, whate'er I fay is deem'd abfurd;
She fcorns my fage advice:—but mark my word,
If to this ball you let the hoyden run,
Your power is ended, and the girl undone."

The patriot knight, by interruption vext,
In his political purfuits perplext,

* Ζευ πατιρ, ἀ νεμεσιζη, ὁρῶν ταδε καρτερα εργα, &c.
ILIAD ε. v. 872. & feq.

While

While he with wrath th' intruding Mifchief eyed,
Stern to the falfe PENELOPE replied:
" Go! teazing prude, ceafe in my ears to vent
Thy envious pride, and peevifh difcontent!
To me of prudence canft thou vainly boaft?
Of all my houfhold, thou haft plagu'd me moft :
The joys thou blameft are thy dear delight,
By day the vifit, and the ball by night :
And, tho' too old a lover to trepan,
Thy midnight dream, thy morning thought, is man.
Wert thou lefs clofely to my blood allied,
Thou fhould'ft, to cure thee of thy canting pride,
Be fent to figh alone o'er purling brooks,
, Scold village maids, and croak to croaking rooks."
    He fpoke indignant: the fly fiend withdrew,
Nor inly griev'd; for well her force fhe knew.
As Indian females, in a jealous hour,
Of fecret poifon try the fubtleft power,
Which fure, tho' flow, corrodes th' unconfcious prey,
And ends its triumph on a diftant day:

Thus

Thus the departing Fury left behind

Her venom, latent in SIR GILBERT's mind.

The hidden mifchief tho' no eye obferves,

He feels it fretting on his alter'd nerves;

But the kind habit of his healthy foul

Still ftruggled hard againft its bafe controul.

Now Spleen's dark vapours, in his bofom hid,

Prompt him the promis'd pleafure to forbid;

Now Love's foft pleadings that dire thought deftroy,

And fave the bloffom of his daughter's joy;

Her envious aunt now ferves him for a jeft,

And gay good-humour reaffumes his breaft.

    While Spleen's dark power now finks, and now
      revives,

. At length the day, th' important day, arrives,

Which in his breaft muft end the clofe debate,

And fix the colour of SERENA's fate.

    Now comes the hour, when the convivial knight

Waits to begin the dinner's chearful rite:

His fond heart ever, with a father's pride,

, Joys to behold his darling at his fide;

                  But

But moſt the abſence of her ſmile he feels
. In the gay ſeaſon of his ſocial meals:
Hence, while for her the rich repaſt attends,
His haſty ſummons to the nymph he ſends:
The happy nymph ſuperior cares induce
To riſk his anger by a raſh excuſe:
She craves his pardon; but, for time diſtreſt,
She ſtill is buſy on her magic veſt;
To range her diamonds in a ſparkling zone,
She begs to ſnatch her ſcanty meal alone.

    The knight in ſullen ſtate begins to dine:
Spleen, like a harpy, flutters o'er his wine:
Inviſible ſhe poiſons every diſh,
Tinging with gall his mutton, fowl, and fiſh.
The more he eats, the more perverſe he grows;
For as his hunger ſunk, his choler roſe.
The cloth remov'd, he cries, with vapours ſick,
The pears are mellow, and the port is thick;
Tho' nicer fruit Pomona never knew,
And his rich wine ſurpaſs'd the ruby's hue!

A thou-

A thoufand times his dizzy brain revolves
A ftern command: now doubts, and now refolves
To bid the nymph defcend, and, difarray'd,
Quit her dear projeĉt of the mafquerade:
· As oft kind nature to his heart recurr'd,
And love parental ftopt the cruel word.

    Mean time, unconfcious of the brooding ftorm,
The nymph exults in her improving form:
Gay is her fmile, as thofe the queen of love
Darts on the Graces in her court above,
While they contrive, with love-infpiring cares,
New modes of beauty for the robe fhe wears.
At length, each duty of the toilet paft,
The glance of triumph on the mirror caft,
Now the light wand our finifh'd Ariel arms;
Glad Jenny glories in her lady's charms;
And gives full utterance, as fhe fmooths her veft,
To the fweet bodings of SERENA's breaft.

    O! lovely bias of the female foul!
Which trembling points to pleafure's diftant pole;

Which

Which with fond truft on flattering hope relies, ⎤
O'erleaps each peril, that in profpect lies, ⎬
And fpringing to the goal, anticipates the prize! ⎦
Such was SERENA's fear-difcarding ftate;
Her eye beheld not the dark frowns of fate:
She only faw, the combat all forgot,
The triumph promis'd as her glorious lot.

Now, eager to difplay her light attire,
The fprightly damfel feeks her fullen fire;
His gloomy brow with fportive air fhe kift:
Ah! how could Spleen that magic lip refift?
That voice, whofe melting mufic might affuage
The fcorpion Anger's felf-tormenting rage?
For ne'er did nature to a fire's embrace
Prefent a filial form of fofter grace;
Or fancy view a fhape of lovelier kind
In the bright mirror of her Shakefpeare's mind.

The fulky fiend, in fpite of all her art,
Had now been banifh'd from the father's heart,
But that, refolv'd her utmoft force to try,
She fummon'd to her aid her old ally,

The

The fiery demon, temper-troubling Gout,

Who finks the lively, and appals the ftout;

Who now, affifting Spleen's malignant aim,

Shoots in quick throbbings through Sir Gil-

    bert's frame.

Thus forely pefter'd by a double foe,

Galling his giddy brain, and burning toe,

The tefty knight, with ftern and fullen air,

Denounc'd his humour to the fhudd'ring fair:

" Go change your drefs! give up this vain delight!

I will not hear of mafquerades to-night:

Your chaperone's inform'd fhe need not wait,

So change your drefs! and fit with me fedate."

   As the proud dame, whofe avaricious glee

Built golden caftles in the rich South Sea,

Gaz'd on her broker, when he told her firft

Her wealth was vanifh'd, and the bubble burft:

So gaz'd the nymph, hearing her fire deftroy

Her airy palace of ideal joy.

Firft her fond thoughts to flattering doubt incline,

And deem the harfh command no fix'd defign,

                       But

Southard del.

Heath sculp.

Published July.1st 1788 by T. Cadell, Strand

But the quick fally of a peevifh word,

. That love revokes, the moment it is heard :

Or haply mirth, in mimic wrath expreft,

A feign'd forbiddance utter'd but in jeft :

To this fhort hope her finking fpirit clung,

. To fee his foftening eyes refute his tongue.

Ah fruitlefs hope ! for there fhe cannot find

The well-known fignals of the friendly mind.

Stern contradiction, with the frown of fate,

On his dark vifage reign'd in fullen ftate ;

Felt in each feature, in each accent fhown,

Lower'd in his look, and thunder'd in his tone.

Hence the warm bofom of the lively fair

Now fhivers with the chill of blank defpair :

Now difappointment's thick'ning fhadows roll

A cloud of horror o'er the darken'd foul ;

And fancy, in a fick delirium toft,

Gives double value to each pleafure loft.

The blafted joys, fhe labours to forget,

Rufh on her mind, and waken keen regret :

Her

Her cheek turns pale—the tear prepares to ſtart,
And palpitation heaves her ſwelling heart.
But here, SOPHROSYNE ! thy guardian aid
Saves from her potent foe the ſinking maid.
Her boſom, into ſtrong emotions thrown,
Now feels the preſſure of thy friendly zone.
Swift thy kind cautions to her ſoul recur,
. More quick to cancel faults, than prone to err.
As the rough ſwell of the inſurgent tides
By the mild impulſe of the moon ſubſides.:
So, by her myſtic monitor repreſt,
The flood of paſſion leaves her lighten'd breaſt,
From her clear brain each cloudy vapour flies,
And joy's bright ray rekindles in her eyes.
Reviving gaiety full luſtre ſpread
O'er all her features, and with ſmiles ſhe ſaid :
" Let others drive to pleaſure's diſtant dome !
Be mine the dearer joy to pleaſe at home !"
Scarce had ſhe ſpoke, when ſhe with ſportive eaſe
Preſt her piano-forte's fav'rite keys,

O'er

O'er fofteft notes her rapid fingers ran,

Sweet prelude to the Air fhe thus began !

Sophrosyne ! thou guard unfeen !

Whofe delicate controul

Can turn the difcord of chagrin

To harmony of foul !

Above the lyre, the lute above,

Be mine thy melting tone,

· Which makes the peace of all we love

The bafis of our own !

So fung the nymph, not uninfpir'd : the fprite

Invok'd fo fondly in the myftic rite,

With richeft mufic fwell'd her warbling throat,

And gave new fweetnefs to her fweeteft note.

As when the feraph Uriel firft begun

His carol to the new-created fun,

The facred echo fhook the vaft profound,

And chaos perifh'd at the potent found :

So,

So, at the magic of SERENA's ſtrain,

Spleen vaniſh'd from her ſire's chaotic brain ;

Whoſe fibres, lighten'd of that load, rejoice

In the dear accents of her dulcet voice.

Much he inclines his mandate to recall,

And ſend the fair-one to the promis'd ball ;

. But ſtubborn pride forbids him to revoke

· The ſolemn ſentence, which ill-humour ſpoke.

Still, conſcious of her power, the nymph prolongs

The ſoft enchantment of her ſoothing ſongs ;

Which his fond mind in firm attention keep,

To his fixt hour of ſupper and of ſleep :

This now arriv'd, the knight, retiring, ſhed

A double bleſſing on his darling's head ;

And with unuſual exultation preſt

His lovely child to his parental breaſt.

Thus while to reſt the happy ſire withdrew,

The nymph, more happy, to her chamber flew ;

And, Jenny now diſmiſs'd, the grateful fair

Breathes to her guardian Sprite this tender prayer :

" Thou

" Thou kind preferver ! whofe attentive zeal
Gives me in this contented hour to feel
That deareft pleafure of a foul refin'd,
The triumph of the felf-corrected mind ;
If, happy in the ftrength thy fmiles impart,
I own thy favour in no thanklefs heart,
Still let me view thy form, fo juftly dear !
Still in kind vifions to thefe eyes appear !
Thy friendly dictates teach me to fulfil !
And let thy aid avert each future ill !"

While fond devotion taught her thus to fpeak,
The foft down finks beneath her lovely cheek,
And fettling on her lips, that fweetly clofe,
Silence, enamour'd, lulls her to repofe.

END OF THE SECOND CANTO.

CANTO

CANTO III.

YE kind tranfporters of th' excurfive foul!
Ye vifions! that, when night enwraps the pole,
The lively wanderer to new worlds convey,
Efcaping from her heavy houfe of clay,
How could the gentle fpirit, foe to ftrife,
Bear without you this coil of waking life?
Its grief-embitter'd cares, its joylefs mirth,
And all the flat realities of earth?
Sweet phantoms! you the glowing hope infpire,
You give to beauty charms, to fancy fire,
When, foaring like the eagle's kindred frame,
The poet dreams of everlafting fame;
Or, tickled by the feather of the dove,
The fofter virgin dreams of endlefs love.
There was a time, when fortune's bright decrees
Were feen to realize fuch dreams as thefe:

Now

Now dangerous vifions the fond mind decoy

Vainly to pant for unexifting joy,

While belles and bards with mournful fighs exclaim,

Mortality has feiz'd both Love and Fame.

    Ah fair SERENA, might the boaft be ours

To clear from fuch a charge thefe heavenly powers !

Bleft ! might thy bard deferve in Fame to fee

A guard as faithful, as Love proves to thee !

Bleft ! if that airy being gild his life,

Who fav'd thee trembling on the brink of ftrife,

And now kind prompter of thy nightly dream,

Fill'd thy rapt fpirit with her facred beam !

For foon as flumber fet thy foul at large,

Thy Guardian Power revifited her charge ;

And, lightly hovering o'er th' illumin'd bed,

. Thus with fond fmiles of approbation faid :

    " Well haft thou paft, fweet maid, one trying
      fcene,

One fiery ordeal of the tyrant Spleen :

             E   Thus,

Thus, my SERENA, may thy force fuſtain
Each harder trial, that may yet remain !
Againſt the fiend to fortify thy ſoul,
By uſeful knowledge of her dark controul,
I come to ſhow thee, what no mortal eye,
Save thine, was e'er permitted to deſcry ;
The realms, where Spleen's infernal agents goad
The ghoſtly tenants of her drear abode.
Now ſummon all thy ſtrength ! throw fear aſide,
And firmly truſt in thy ætherial guide !"

    She ſpoke: and thro' the night's ſurrounding
       ſhade
Th' obedient nymph, not unappall'd, convey'd ;
Thro' long, long traĉts of darkneſs, on they paſt
With ſpeed, that ſtruck the trembling maid aghaſt,
Till now, recovering by degrees, ſhe found
Her ſoft foot preſs upon the ſolid ground.
Encourag'd by her guide, at length ſhe tries
To ſearch the gloomy ſcene, with anxious eyes.

                     " Thro'

* " Thro' me ye pafs to Spleen's terrific dome,
Thro' me, to Difcontent's eternal home :
Thro' me, to thofe, who fadden'd human life,
By fullen humour or vexatious ftrife ;
And here, thro' fcenes of endlefs vapours hurl'd,
Are punifh'd in the forms they plagued the world ;
Juftly they feel no joy, who none beftow,
All ye who enter, every hope forego !"
O'er an arch'd cavern, rough with horrid ftone,
On which a feeble light, by flashes, fhone,
Thefe characters, that chill'd her foul with dread,
SERENA, fixt in filent wonder, read.
As fhe began to fpeak, her voice was drown'd
By the fhrill echo of far other found :

* Per me fi va nella citta dolente,
    Per me fi va nell' eterno dolore,
    Per me fi va tra la perduta gente,
    * * * * * * * * *
    Lafciate ogni fperanza, voi ch' intrate.
Quefte parole di colore ofcuro
    Vid' io fcritte al fommo d'una porta.
                    DANTE, Inferno. 3.

E 2   Forth

Forth from the portal lamentable cries

Of wailing infants, without number, rife.

Compaffion to this poor and piteous flock

Led the foft maid ftill nearer to the rock.

The pining band within fhe now efpied,

And, touch'd with tender indignation, cried,

" How could thefe little forms, of life fo brief,

Deferve this dire abode of lafting grief ?"

" —Well may thy gentle heart be fore concern'd

At fight fo moving," the mild Sprite return'd :

" Thou feeft in thofe, whofe wailings wound thy
   ears,

The puny progeny of modern peers :

Their fires, by avarice or ambition led,

Aliens to love, approach'd the nuptial bed ;

With proud indifference, and with cold diftafte,

Their homely brides reluctantly embrac'd,

And by fuch union gave difaftrous birth

To thefe poor pale incumbrances of earth,

Who, bred in vanity, with pride their dower,

Were Spleen's fure victims from their natal hour,

        And

And in their ſplendid cradles pul'd and pin'd,

Till Fate their ill-ſpun thread of life untwin'd,

And to this veſtibule convey'd their ghoſts,

To form the van-guard of th' infernal hoſts.

But let not pity's ineffectual charm

Impede thy progreſs, or thy ſtrength diſarm !

Follow and fear not ! guarded by my care

From all the phantoms that around thee glare.''

   She ſpoke ; and enter'd, ere the nymph replied,

A paſs, that open'd in the cavern's ſide,

Low, dark, and rocky—with her body bent,

SERENA follow'd down the dire deſcent.

A ſudden light ſoon ſtruck her dazzled view ;

But 'twas a light of ſuch infernal hue,

As double horror to the darkneſs gave,

With dread reflection from a duſky wave.

Round a black water tatter'd ſpectres ſtand,

With each a tiny taper in its hand ;

Fierce mendicants ! who ſtrive ſome alms to win

From the fair wanderer, with inceſſant din.

             The

, The guardian Spirit faw SERENA grieve,

To hear of wants fhe knew not to relieve ;

And to the generous nymph in pity cries :

" The gulf of Indolence before us lies,

O'er whofe dull flood, to which no bank is feen,

A boat muft waft thee to the dome of Spleen.

Thefe pallid figures, that around thee prefs,

And haunt thee with importunate diftrefs,

On earth were beggars of each different clafs,

Tho' blended here in one promifcuous mafs.

The poor, who fpurn'd kind induftry's controul,

· The rich, who begg'd from penury of foul :

Both by their abject pride alike debas'd,

Blafphem'd that nature, which they both difgrac'd,

And, hither by the fullen fiend convey'd,

Here ftill they ply their ineffectual trade ;

In chafe of each new paffenger they run,

Condemn'd to beg from all, to gain by none.

But from thefe wretches turn thy fruitlefs care !

Behold the gulf before thee, and beware !

Nor

Nor touch the ſtream, which mortal ſenſe o'ercomes,

And by its baleful charm the ſoul benumbs !"

" — Can mortal paſs !" the ſhudd'ring nymph replied,

" This ſullen, ſlow, unnavigable tide,

In whoſe black current this enormous mound

Of ſhapeleſs ſtone appears, this horrid bound,

That ſeems an everlaſting guard to keep

O'er the dull waters, that beneath it creep ?"

While yet ſhe ſpoke, with a reſounding ſhock,

Forth from the arch of the impending rock,

Which o'er the murmuring eddy hung ſo low,

The lazy river ſcarce had room to flow,

Of rude conſtruction, and in rougheſt plight,

A boat now iſſued to SERENA's ſight ;

An empty boat, that ſlowly to the ſhore

Advanc'd, without the aid of ſail or oar ;

Self-mov'd it ſeem'd, but ſoon the nymph beheld

A griſly figure, who the ſtern impell'd.

Wading

Wading behind, the horrid form appear'd ;

Above the water his ftrong arm he rear'd,

And crofs the creeping flood the crazy veffel fteer'd.

The heavenly Sprite obferv'd her trembling ward,

Whofe growing fears the hideous pafs abhorr'd,

And cheering thus fhe fpake : " This fpectre boafts

The chief dominion of thefe dreary coafts :

To him, thy pilot, without dread confign,

And place thy body in his bark fupine !

So thro' this arching rock thou'lt pafs alone,

Safe from the perils of th' incumbent flone :

Embark undaunted !—on the farther fide

Thou'lt furely find me, thy unfailing guide.

Nor let this pilot raife thy groundlefs dread,

This fullen Charon of the froward dead,

A phantom, never bleft with human life,

Tho' oft on earth his noxious power is rife ;

And in that region, ne'er from error free,

The words he dictates are affign'd to me.

Obferve

Stothard del   Heath sculp.

London Publish'd Sept. 2. 1788 by T. Cadell. Strand

Obferve this fiend, that Nature fcorn'd to frame,

. Offspring of Pride, and Apathy his name !

Paffions he ne'er can feel, and ne'er impart,

⌄ A mifcreated imp, without a heart ;

In place of which, his fubtle parent pinn'd

A bladder, fill'd with circulating wind,

Which feems with mimic life the mafs to warm,

And gives falfe vigour to his bloated form.

But place thee in the boat his arms direct,

My love fhall watch thee, and my power protect."

So fpake the friendly Sprite ; th' obedient maid

Her form along the narrow veffel laid :

But oh ! what terrors fhake her tender foul,

As from the fhore the bark begins to roll,

And, fever'd from her friend, her eyes difcern

The fteering fpectre wading at the ftern !

Far ftronger fears her refolution melt,

Than thofe, which erft the bard of Florence felt,

When, by the honour'd fhade of Virgil led

Thro' all the dreary circles of the dead,

Hell's

Hell's fierceft demons threaten'd to divide
The living poet from his fhadowy guide ;
And bade him, friendlefs, and alone, return,
Thro' the dire horrors of the dark fojourn.
Not long the lovely fair one's terrors laft ;
For fafely thro' th' impending rock fhe paft :
And flow advancing to the gloomy ftrand,
The fullen pilot brings her fafe to land.
There, fondly hovering on her guardian plumes,
The heavenly Monitor her charge refumes ;
And fmiling, leads along the rocky road,
Whofe windings open into Spleen's abode.

   Thou queen of fhades ! whofe fpirit-damping fpell
Too oft is feen the poet's pride to quell,
May I, unpunifh'd by thy fubtle power,
Dare to difplay thy fubterranean bower,
And to this wond'ring upper world explain
The fhadowy horrors of thy fecret reign ?

   Entering beneath a wide fantaftic arch,
Round the drear circuit of the dome they march ;

Which

Which a pale flash from many a fiery fprite
Frequent illumes with intermitting light;
Such, as on earth, to Superftition's eye,
Denounces ruin from the northern fky,
While fhe difcerns, amid the nightly glare,
Armies embattled in the blazing air.

　　Around the nymph unnumber'd phantoms glide;
Here fwell the bloated race of bulky Pride:
In clofe and horrid union, there appear
The wilder progeny of frantic Fear;
Mif-fhapen monfters! whofe ftupendous frame
• Abhorrent Nature has refus'd to name.
Here, in cameleon colours, lightly flit
The motley offspring of diforder'd Wit.
All things prodigious the wide cave contain'd,
And forms, beyond what fable ever feign'd:
But, as the worm, that on the dewy green
Springs half to view, and half remains unfeen,
Perceiving near its cell a human tread,
Slinks back to earth, and hides its timid head:

　　　　　　　　　　　　　　So,

So, where the heavenly Spirit deign'd to lead,
The ſtartled ſpeƈtres from her ſtep recede ;
And, as abaſh'd they from her eye retire,
Sink into miſt, or melt in fluid fire.

High on an ebon throne, ſuperbly wrought
With each fierce figure of fantaſtic thought,
In a deep cove, where no bright beam intrudes,
O'er her black ſchemes the ſullen empreſs broods.
The ſcreech-owl's mingled with the raven's plume
Shed o'er her furrow'd brows an awful gloom ;
A garb, that glares with ſtripes of lurid flame,
Wraps in terrific pomp her haggard frame ;
Round her a ſerpent, as her zone, is roll'd,
Which, writhing, ſtings itſelf in every fold.

Near her pavilion, in barbaric ſtate,
Four mutes the mandates of their queen await.
From ſickly Fancy bred, by ſullen Sloth,
Both parents' curſe, yet pamper'd ſtill by both,
Firſt ſtands Diſeaſe ; an hag of magic power,
Varying her frightful viſage every hour,

Her

Her horrors heightening, as thofe changes laft,

And each new form more hideous than the paft.

Detraction next, a fhapelefs fiend, appears,

Whofe fhrivell'd hand a mifty mirror rears;

Fram'd by malignant Art, th' infernal toy

Inverts the lovely mien of fmiling Joy,

Robs rofeate Beauty of attractive grace,

And gives a ftepdame's frown to Nature's face.

The third in place, but with a fiercer air,

See the true Gorgon Difappointment glare!

By whofe petrific power Delight's o'erthrown;

And Hope's warm heart becomes an icy ftone.

Laft, in a gorgeous robe, that, ill beftow'd,

Bows her mean body by its cumbrous load,

. Stands fretful Difcontent, of fiends the worft,

By dignity debas'd, by bleffings curft,

Who poifons Pleafure with the foureft leaven,

And makes a hell of Love's ecftatic heaven.

The guide celeftial, near this ghaftly group,

Perceiv'd her tender charge with terror droop:

" Fear

" Fear not, fweet maid," fhe cries, " my fteps
    purfue !

Nor gaze too long on this infernal crew !

Turn from Detraction's fafcinating glafs !

In filence crofs the throne ! obferve, and pafs !

Beyond this dome, the palace of the queen,

Her empire winds thro' many a dreary fcene,

Where fhe torments, as their deferts require,

Her various victims, that on earth expire ;

Each clafs apart : for in a different cell

The fierce, the fretful, and the fullen dwell :

Thefe fhalt thou flightly view, in vapours hurl'd,

And fwiftly then regain thy native world.

But firft remark, within that ample nich,

With every quaint device of fplendor rich,

Yon phantom, who, from vulgar eyes withdrawn,

Appears to ftretch in one eternal yawn :

Of empire here he holds the tottering helm,

Prime minifter in Spleen's difcordant realm,

The pillar of her fpreading ftate, and more,

Her darling offspring, whom on earth fhe bore ;

                                    For,

For, as on earth his wayward mother ſtray'd,

Grandeur, with eyes of fire, her form ſurvey'd,

And with ſtrong paſſion ſtarting from his throne,

Unloos'd the ſullen queen's reluĉtant zone.

From his embrace, conceiv'd in moody joy,

Roſe the round image of a bloated boy :

His nurſe was Indolence ; his tutor Pomp,

Who kept the child from every childiſh romp ;

They rear'd their nurſling to the bulk you ſee,

And his proud parents call'd their imp ENNUI.

This realm he rules, and in ſuperb attire

Viſits each earthly palace of his ſire :

A thouſand ſhapes he wears, now pert, now prim,

Purſues each grave conceit, or idle whim ;

In arms, in arts, in government engages,

With monarchs, poets, politicians, ſages ;

But drops each work, the moment it's begun,

. And, trying all things, can accompliſh none :

Yet o'er each rank, and age, and ſex, his ſway

Spreads undiſcern'd, and makes the world his prey.

The

. The light coquet, amid flirtation, fighs,

To find him lurk in Pleafure's vain difguife ;

And the grave nun difcovers, in her cell,

That holy water but augments his fpell.

, As the ftrange monfter of the ferpent breed,

That haunts, as travellers tel!, the marfhy mead,

Devours each nobler beaft, tho' firmly grown

To fize and ftrength fuperior to his own ;—

For on the grazing horfe, or larger bull,

Subtly he fprings, of dark faliva full,

With fwiftly-darting tongue his prey anoints

With venom, potent to diffolve its joints,

And, while its bulk in liquid poifon fwims,

Swallows its melting bone and fluid limbs :—

So this Ennui, this wonder-working elf,

Can vanquifh powers far mightier than himfelf :

Nor Wit nor Science foar his reach above,

And oft he feizes on fuccefsful Love.

Of all the radiant hoft who lend their aid

To light mankind thro' life's bewildering fhade,

Bright

Bright Charity alone, with cloudlefs ray,

. May boaft exemption from his baleful fway :

Hafte then, fweet nymph, nor let us longer roam

Round the drear circle of this dangerous dome !

Left e'en thy guide, entangled in his fpell,

Should fail to guard thee from a fiend fo fell !"

 So fpeaking, the kind Spirit's anxious care

Led from the palace the attentive fair,

And, winding through a paffage dark and rude,

Thus the mild monitor her fpeech renew'd :

" 'Gainft fear and pity now thy bofom fteel,

For fights more horrible I now reveal !

Spleen's tortur'd victims view with dauntlefs eyes ;

For lo ! her penal realms before thee rife !"

The nymph advancing faw, with mute amaze,

A difmal, deep, enormous dungeon blaze.

Stones of red fire the hideous wall compos'd ;

And maffive gates the horrid confine clos'd.

Th' infernal portrefs of this doleful dome,

With fiery lips, that fwell'd with poifonous foam,

F   Pale

Pale Difcord, rag'd; with whofe tormenting tongue,
Thro' all its caves th' extenfive region rung :
A living vulture was the fury's creft;
And in her hand a rattlefnake fhe preft,
Whofe angry joints inceffantly were heard
To found defiance to the fcreaming bird.

    " The boundlefs depth of this dire prifon holds
The untam'd fpirits of imperious fcolds :
Nor think that females only fill the cave !
Male termagants have liv'd, and here they rave.
All of each fex are pent within this pale,
Who knew no ufe of language, but to rail."
Thus to her charge exclaim'd the heavenly guide,
And, as fhe fpoke, the portals open'd wide,
And to th' obfervance of the fhuddering maid,
Th' immeafurable den was all difplay'd.
But oh ! what various noifes from within
Fill the vext air with one ftupendous din !
Mourning's deep groan, and anger's furious call,
Terror's loud cry, and affeCtation's fquall,

                         The

, The fob of paffion, the hyfteric fcream,

And fhrieks of frenzy, in its fierce extreme !

In this wild uproar every found's combin'd,

That ftuns the fenfes, and diftracts the mind.

" Mark" (to the nymph Sophrosyne began)

" The fierce Xantippe flaming in the van,

The vafe, fhe emptied on the fage's head,

Hangs o'er her own, a different fhower to fhed ;

For, drop by drop, diftilling liquid fire,

It fills the vixen with new tropes of ire.

Beyond the Grecian dame extend your view,

And mark the fpectre of a modern fhrew !

She, who whene'er fhe din'd, with furious look,

Spurn'd her nice food, and bellow'd at her cook,

Here juftly feels a culinary rack,

. Bound like Ixion, to a whirling jack."

Serena gaz'd, but foon fhe turn'd away,

Mute with difguft, and fhuddering with difmay.

" To fcenes lefs hideous let us now repair !"

(Said the kind guard of the dejected fair)

And,

And, cheering her faint charge, her ftep fhe led
To the near dwelling of the fretful dead.

Of dufky adamant the dungeon rofe;
A dingy mirror its dark fides compofe,
Reflecting, with a thoufand quaint grimaces,
The pale inhabitants' diftorted faces.
" Here, like a dame of quality array'd,
Sits Peevifhnefs, prefiding o'er the fhade,
And frowning at her own uncomely mien,
Whofe coarfe reflection on the wall is feen.
A fnarling lap-dog her right-hand reftrains,
Her lap an infant porcupine contains,
Which, while her fondnefs tries its wrath to ftill,
Wounds her each moment with a pointed quill.
The froward fpirits here in durance fret,
Whofe tefty life was one continued pet ;
Here they in trifles that vexation find,
Which teaz'd on earth their irritated mind.
Obferve the phantom, who with eyes afkance
Still to the mirror turns her eager glance !

See !

See ! to her cheek, inceſſant as ſhe turns,

Her vex'd blood ruſhes, and her viſage burns.

Beauty for laſting bliſs had form'd the maid ;

Love to her charms his faithful homage paid ;

But, all this ſwelling tide of joy to check,

A fatal freckle riſes on her neck :

Her ſoft coſmetics the griev'd nymph applies,

Succeſs attends her, and the freckle dies :

But ah ! this victory avails her not ;

She finds an hydra in the teazing ſpot :

Faſt as one flies, another ſtill ſucceeds,

. And with eternal food her fretful humour feeds.

　　Near to the nymph, in a more moody fit,

See the pale phantom of a peeviſh wit !

Mark with what frowns his eager eyes peruſe,

Wet from the preſs, three Critical Reviews !

With wounded vanity's diſtracting rage

How rapidly he runs thro' every page !

He finds ſome honours laviſh'd on his verſe,

And joy's faint gleams his gloomy ſpirit pierce.

But

But oh! too foon thefe feeble fparks decay;

. And keen vexation reaffumes her prey.

Hating reproof, in every fibre fore,

One cenfur'd particle torments him more,

More than a hundred happier lines delight,

Which liberal favour condefcends to cite.

But time will fail us, if we paufe to view

The various torments of the tefty crew;

. Thefe wretched chymifts, whofe o'erheated brain

- Extracts from nothing a fubftantial pain.

Yet, ere to different diftricts we advance,

Take of one fretful tribe a tranfient glance!

Their unfufpected punifhments fupply

A leffon, ufeful to the female eye.

Spleen's livelieft agent here beguiles the gay,

· Fair to attract, and flattering to betray."

As thus the kind æthereal guardian fpoke,

Within a rock, whence plaintive murmurs broke,

She touch'd a fecret fpring, whofe power was fuch,

Two jarring doors unfolded at the touch,

And,

And, with the charms of regal fplendor bright,'

A chearful banquet fparkles to the fight.

Viands fo light, fo elegantly grac'd,

Might tempt e'en Temperance herfelf to tafte ;

For fruits alone compos'd th' enticing treat,

Fair to the eye, and to the palate fweet.

In fuch bright juice the peach and cherry fwim,

As make the topaz and the ruby dim.

Here crown'd with every flower, and gaily dreft

In all the glitter of a Gallic veft,

Whofe ample folds her loathfome body fcreen'd,

A child of luxury reigns, a fubtle fiend !

. Who, with a grace that every heart allures,

Smiles on the luftre of her rich *liqueurs.*

Her fatal fmiles their utmoft power exert

To poifon beauty at her dire deffert ;

. To blaft the rofe that health's bright cheek adorns,

. And fill each feftive heart with latent thorns :

For the fly fiend, of every art poffeft,

Steals on th' affection of her female gueft ;

And,

And, by her foft addrefs feducing each,

Eager fhe plies them with a brandy peach :

They with keen lip the lufcious fruit devour ;

But fwiftly feel its peace-deftroying power.

Quick thro' each vein new tides of frenzy roll:

All evil paffions kindle in the foul,

Drive from each feature every chearful grace,

And glare ferocious in the fallow face ;

The wounded nerves in furious conflict tear,

Then fink, in blank dejection and defpair.

Effects more dire, thus tempting to deceive,

The apple wrought not in the foul of Eve ;

. Howe'er difguis'd, in jelly or in jam,

Spleen has no poifon furer than a dram.

    " But hafte we now" (the heavenly leader cries)

" To where this penal world's laft wonder lies !"

She fpoke ; and led the nymph thro' deeper dells,

Low-murmuring vaults, and horror-breathing cells.

And now they pafs a perforated cage,

Where rancorous fpectres without number rage.

                            " Avert

" Avert thine eye !" (the heavenly Spirit faid)

" Nor view thefe abject tribes of envious dead !

Who pin'd to hear the voice of truth proclaim

A fifter's beauty, or a brother's fame !

Tho' crown'd with all profperity imparts,

High in their various ranks, and feveral arts ;

Yet, meanly funk by envy's bafe controul,

They died in that confumption of the foul ;

And here, thro' bars that twifted adders make,

And the long volumes of th' envenom'd fnake,

O'er this dark road they dart an anxious eye,

Still envying every fiend that flutters by.

Pafs ! and regard them not!"—Th' attentive maid

In filent tremor the beheft obey'd.

This dungeon croft, her weary feet fhe drags

Thro' winding caverns, and o'er icy crags :

Soul-chilling damps in the dark paffage reign,

Which iffues on a vaft and dreary plain,

Fann'd by no breezes, with no verdure crown'd ;

The black horizon is its only bound.

And

And now advancing, in a drizzly mift,

Thro' fullen phantoms, hating to exift,

SERENA fpies, high o'er his fubjects plac'd,

The ghaftly tyrant of the gloomy wafte.

Murmuring he fits upon a rocking ftone,

Th' unftable bafe of his ill-founded throne:

Hideous his face, and horrible his frame,

Mifanthropy the grifly monfter's name!

Him to fierce Pride, with raging paffion fore,

The frowning gorgon, Difappointment, bore;

On earth detefted, and by heaven abhorr'd,

Of this drear wild he reigns the moody lord.

Few are the fubjects of his wafte domain,

And fcarce a female in his frightful train,

· Except one changing corps of ancient prudes:

Reluctant here the prying band intrudes.

Each, who on earth, behind her artful fan,

· Feign'd coarfe averfion to the creature man,

Is doom'd, in this dark region, to abide

Some tranfient pains for hypocritic pride.

                                        Here

Here ever-during chains thofe fcoffers bind,

Whofe writings deaden and debafe the mind;

Who mock creation with injurious fcorn,

. And feel a fancied void in plenty's horn.

 In his right-hand, an emblem of his cares,

. A branch of aconite the monarch bears;

And thofe four phantoms, who this region haunt,

He feeds with berries from this deadly plant;

For, ftrange to tell! tho' fever'd from its root,

. The bough ftill blackens with fucceffive fruit.

The tribes, who tafte it, burft into a fit

Of raving mockery and rancorous wit;

And, pleas'd their tyrant's ghaftly fmile to court,

By vile diftortions make him various fport.

The frantic rabble, who his fway confefs,

Before his throne an hideous puppet drefs;

When in unfeemly rags they have array'd

The image, from their own dark femblance made,

In horrid gambols round their work they throng,

With antic dance and rude difcordant fong;

Satire's

Satire's rank offals on the block they fling,

And call it nature, to delight their king :

While in their features he exults to fee

The frowns of torture, mixt with grins of glee.

For, as thefe abject toils engage the crew,

Their own grim idol darkens to their view ;

Wide and more wide its horrid ftature fpreads,

And o'er the tribe new confternation fheds :

For each forgets, in his bewilder'd gaze,

'Tis but a monfter, which he help'd to raife.

As o'er its form their dizzy glances roll,

It ftrikes a chearlefs damp thro' all the foul.

Vainly to fhun the baleful fight they try,

It draws for ever the reluctant eye :

At each review with deeper dread they ftart ;

A colder chaos numbs each freezing heart.

No mutual confidence, no friendly care,

Relieves the panic they are doom'd to bear ;

For as they fhrink abforb'd in wild affright,

When each to each inclines his wounded fight,

They

They feel, for focial comfort, four difguft,
. And all the fullen anguifh of diftruft.

Around thefe wretches in the drear abode,
The ghaftly grinning fiend Derifion rode,
Who to their wayward minds on earth fupplied
. Perverted ridicule's malignant tide.
His fteed of Pegafus the femblance bore;
But with falfe wings, that knew not how to foar:
Where'er he pafs'd, with mifchief in his look,
A founding whip of knotted fnakes he fhook;
And laugh'd in lafhing each pretended fage,
Whofe malice wore the mafk of moral rage.
An uncouth bugle his left-hand difplay'd,
From a grey monkey's fkull by Cunning made,
And form'd to pour, in harmony's defpite,
Sounds that each jarring fenfe of pain excite:
And now his livid lips this bugle blew;
Thro' every den the piercing difcord flew:
The fiends all anfwer'd in one hideous yell,
And in a fearful trance SERENA fell.

Hence

Hence from the lovely nymph her senses fled,

Till, thro' the parted curtains of her bed,

The amorous sun, who now began to rise,

. Kist, with a sportive beam, her opening eyes.

END OF THE THIRD CANTO.

CANTO

CANTO IV.

HAIL, thou enlighten'd globe of human joy !
Where focial cares the foften'd heart employ :
What cheering rays of vital comfort roll
In thy bright regions o'er the refcued foul,
Which, 'fcaping from the dark domain of Spleen,
Springs with new warmth to thy attractive fcene !
Once more I blefs thy pleafure-breathing gale,
And gaze enchanted on thy flowery vale,
Where fmiling innocence, and ardent youth,
Sport hand in hand with beauty and with truth.
Sport on, fweet revellers ! in rofy bowers,
Safe from th' intrufion of all evil powers !
Ah fruitlefs wifh of the benignant Mufe,
Which to this chequer'd world the Fates refufe !
For round its precincts many an ugly fprite
Speeds undifcern'd to poifon pure delight :

Amidft

Amidſt the foremoſt of this haggard band,
Unwearied poſter of the ſea and land,
Wrapt in dark miſts, malignant Scandal flies,
. While Envy's poiſon'd breath the buoyant gale ſup-
      plies.
· Tho' SHERIDAN, with ſhafts of comic wit,
Pierc'd, and expos'd her to the laughing pit,
Th' immortal hag ſtill wears her paper crown,
The dreaded empreſs of the idle town :
O'erleaping her prerogative of old,
To ſink the noble, to defame the bold ;—
In chaſe of worth to ſlip the dogs of ſtrife,
. Thro' all the ample range of public life ;—
The tyrant now, that ſanctuary burſt
Where happineſs by privacy is nurſt,
Her fury riſing as her powers encreaſe,
O'erturns the altars of domeſtic peace.
Pleas'd in her dark and gall-diſtilling cloud
The ſportive form of innocence to ſhroud,
Beauty's young train her baleful eyes ſurvey,
To mark the faireſt, as her favourite prey.

                              Hence,

Hence, fweet SERENA, while thy fpirit ftray'd
Round the deep realms of fubterranean fhade,
This keeneft agent of th' infernal powers
On earth was bufied, in thofe tranquil hours,
To blaft thy peace, and poifon'd darts to aim
Againft the honour of thy fpotlefs name:
For Scandal, reftlefs fiend, who never knows
The balmy bleffing of an hour's repofe,
Worn, yet unfated with her daily toil,
In her bafe work confumes the midnight oil.
O'er fiercer fiends when heavy flumbers creep,
When wearied avarice and ambition fleep,
Scandal is vigilant, and keen to fpread
The plagues that fpring from her prolific head.
On truth's fair bafis fhe her falfehood builds,
With tinfel fentiment its furface gilds;
To nightly labour from their dark abodes
The demons of the groaning prefs fhe goads,
And fmiles to fee their rapid art fupply
Ten thoufand wings to every infant lie.

G

In

In triumph now behold the hag applaud
Her keen and fav'rite imp, ingenious Fraud,
Her quick compofitor, whofe flying hand
Has clofd the paragraph fhe keenly plann'd.
No nymph fhe nam'd, yet mark'd her vile intent,
That dulnefs could not mifs the name fhe meant :
In fatire's tints the injur'd fair fhe drew,
In form an angel, but in foul a Jew.

It chanc'd her fire among his friends inroll'd
A wealthy fenator, infirm and old ;
Who, dup'd too early by a generous heart,
Rafhly affum'd a mifanthropic part :
Tho' peevifh fancies would his mind incruft,
Good-nature's image lurk'd beneath their ruft ;
And gay SERENA, with that fportive wit
Which heals the folly that it deigns to hit,
Would oft the ficknefs of his foul beguile,
And teach the fullen humorift to fmile ;
Pleas'd by her virtuous frolics to affuage
The mental anguifh of diftemper'd age.

This

This ancient friend, in a farcastic sketch,

Was mark'd by Scandal as a monied wretch,

For whom the young, yet mercenary fair

Had subtly spread a matrimonial snare.

With such base matter. more diffusely wrought,

The spirit-piercing paragraph was fraught,

O'er which with glee the eye of Scandal glar'd,

Which for the opening press herself prepar'd;

She on the types her inky wad let fall,

And smear'd each letter with her bitterest gall;

The press, whose ready gripe the charge receives,

Stamps it successive on ten thousand leaves,

Which pil'd in heaps impatient seem to lie,

They only wait the dawn of day to fly.

　　Now, as the child, in lonely chamber laid,

Mute in the dark, and of itself afraid,

When, haply conscious of the pain it feels,

The watchful mother to its pillow steals,

Springs to her breast, and shakes off all alarms,

Feeling its safety in her fostering arms:

　　　　　　　　With

With fuch quick joy, in innocence as young,

The foft SERENA from her pillow fprung,

. Pleas'd to awake from her terrific dream,

And feel the chearful fun's returning beam.

Eager fhe rofe, in bufy thought, nor ftaid

The wonted fummons of her punctual maid,

And as her own fair hands adjuft her veft,

The guardian cincture flutters on her breaft;

For fondly, when fhe wak'd, or when fhe flept,

Still round her heart th' important zone fhe kept.

Thou happy girdle! to thy charge be juft!

Firm be thy threads, and faithful to their truft;

For hours approach, when all the ftores they hide

Of magic virtue, muft be ftrongly tried!—

Now, while her kind domeftic heart intends

To pleafe her early fire, the nymph defcends;

But fleep, who left the fair with fudden flight,

With late wings hover'd o'er the good old knight;

And the chill circle of the lone faloon

Informs the fhiv'ring maid fhe rofe too foon.

'Tis

. 'Tis true, attentive John's unfailing care

Began the rites of breakfaſt to prepare ;

But yet no fires on the cold altar burn,

No ſmoke ariſes from the ſilver urn,

And the blank tea-board, where no viands lay,

Only ſupplied the paper of the day.

.   Tho' mild SERENA's peace-devoted mind

The keen debate of politics declin'd,

And heard with cold contempt, or generous hate,

The frauds of party and the lies of ſtate ;

Nor car'd much more for faſhion's looſe intrigues,

Than factious bickerings or foreign leagues ;

Yet, while ſhe ſaunters idle and alone,

Her careleſs eyes are on the paper thrown.

As ſome gay youth, whom ſportive friends engage

To view the furious ourang in his cage,

If while amus'd he ſees the monſter grin,

And truſts too careleſs to the bolts within,

If the ſly beaſt, as near the grate he draws,

Tear him unguarded with projected paws,

Starts at the wound, and feels his bofom thrill
With pain and wonder at the fudden ill:
So did SERENA ftart, fo wildly gaze,
In fuch mixt pangs of anguifh and amaze,
. Feeling the wound which Scandal had defign'd
To lacerate her mild and modeft mind.
Startled, as one who from electric wire
Unheeding catches unfufpected fire,
. She reads, then almoft doubts that fhe has read,
And thinks fome vifion hovers round her head.
Now, her fixt eye fome ftriking words confine,
And now fhe darts it thrice thro' every line;
Nor could amazement more her fenfes fhake,
Had every letter been a gorgon's fnake.
Now rifing indignation takes its turn,
And her flufh'd cheeks with tingling blufhes burn,
With reftlefs motion and with many a frown,
Thro' the wide room fhe paces up and down:
Now, mufing, makes a momentary ftand,
The fatal paper fluttering in her hand.

So

So the fhy bird, by cruel fportfmen fprung,

And by their random fire feverely ftung,

Scar'd, not difabled, by the diftant wound,

Now trembling flies, now fkims along the ground,

Now vainly tries, in fome fequefter'd fpot,

From her gor'd breaft to fhake the galling fhot.

 Ye tender nymphs! whofe kindling fouls would
   flame,

Touch'd, like SERENA's, by injurious blame,

O let your quick and kindred fpirits form

A vivid picture of the mental ftorm

In which fhe labour'd, and whofe force to paint

The Mufe's ftrongeft tints appear too faint;

In fympathetic thought her fuffering fee!

But O, for ever from fuch wrongs be free!

 Her faithful girdle try'd its power to fave,

And oft a monitory impulfe gave;

Still unregarded, ftill unfelt, it preft

With ufelefs energy her heaving breaft,

Her mind, forgetful of the magic zone,

Full of the burning fhaft by Scandal thrown,

With blended notes of forrow and difdain,

Thus in diforder'd language vents its pain :—

" Had malice dar'd my honour to defame,

The felf-refuted lie had loft its aim :

But here the world, deceiv'd by fland'rous art,

. Muft think SERENA has a venal heart."

A venal heart ! at that detefted found,

In fwelling anguifh her funk voice was drown'd.

. Now was a fearful crifis of her fate :

Diftended now by paffion's growing weight,

And for its miftrefs fill'd with confcious dread,

The magic girdle crack'd thro' every thread,

And fnapp'd perchance by Scandal's force accurft,

From her full heart the guardian zone had burft,

And, fpite of all the virtues of the fair,

The fpell of happinefs had funk in air,

But that SOPHROSYNE, whofe friendly fear

Timely forefaw this trial too fevere,　　.

An early fuccour gain'd from fecret love,

. From the fell kite to fnatch the falling dove.

As

As Nature ſtudies, in her wide domain,
To blend ſome antidote with every bane ;
Thus her kind aid the friendly power contriv'd,
That, from the quarter whence the wound arriv'd,
There flow'd, the anguiſh of that wound to calm,
A ſoothing, ſoft, and medicinal balm.
As in her agitated hand the fair
Wav'd the looſe paper with diſorder'd air,
In capitals ſhe ſaw SERENA flame :
She bluſh'd, ſhe ſhudder'd, as ſhe view'd the name ;
Her ready fears ſubſide in new ſurpriſe,
And eager thus ſhe reads with lighten'd eyes :

" Go, faithful ſonnet, to SERENA ſay
What charms peculiar in her features reign :
A ſtranger, whom her glance may ne'er ſurvey,
Pays her this tribute in no flattering ſtrain.
Tell her, the bard, in beauty's wide domain,
Has ſeen a virgin cheek as richly glow,

A boſom,

A bofom, where the blue meandring vein
  Sheds as foft luftre thro' the lucid fnow,
Eyes, that as brightly flafh with joy and youth,
  And locks, that like her own luxuriant flow:
Then fay, for then fhe cannot doubt thy truth,
  That the wide earth no female form can fhow
Where nature's legend fo diftinctly tells,
  In this fair fhrine a fairer fpirit dwells."

With curious wonder the reviving maid
View'd this fond homage to her beauty paid;
A fecond glance o'er every line fhe caft,
And half pronounc'd and half fupprefs'd the laft,
While modeft pleafure, and ingenuous pride,
Her burning cheek with deeper crimfon dy'd.
  O Praife! thy language was by heaven defign'd
As manna to the faint bewilder'd mind:
Beauty and diffidence, whofe hearts rejoice
In the kind comfort of thy cheering voice,

                      In

Stothard del   Sharp sculp.

London Published Sept.r 1.st 1788. by T. Cadell Strand

In this wild wood of life, wert thou not nigh,

Muſt, like the wandering babes, lie down and die:

But thy ſweet accents wake new vital powers,

And make this thorny path a path of flowers:

As oil on ocean's troubled waters ſpread,

Smooths the rough billow to a level bed,

The ſoothing rhyme thus ſoften'd into reſt

The painful tumult of SERENA's breaſt.

 Now, to herſelf reſtor'd, the conſcious maid

The lurking fiend's inſidious ſnare ſurvey'd;

Her nerves, with grateful trepidation, own

A ſlighter preſſure from the faithful zone;

And in fond thought ſhe breathes a thankful prayer

For her ætherial guardian's conſtant care;

Yet with a keen deſire her boſom glow'd,

To hear from whom the gentle ſonnet flow'd;

But kind SOPHROSYNE, who watch'd unſeen,

To ſhield her votary from the wiles of Spleen,

As friendly love had fixt a future time,

When to reveal the ſecret of the rhyme,

Strove

Strove till that hour her fancy to reftrain,

. Nor let her anxious wifhes rife to pain.

As gaiety's frefh tide began to roll,

Faft in the fwelling channel of her foul,

The good old knight defcends, tho' eager, flow,

The gout ftill tingling in his tender toe ;

And now, paternal falutations paft,

His eyes he keenly on the paper caft,

While his fweet daughter, with attentive grace,

Before him flies his ready cup to place ;

For tea and politics alternate fhare,

In friendly rivalfhip, his morning care.

Tho' fmooth as oil the knight's good-humour flows,

When the mild breeze of pleafant fortune blows,

Yet, quick to catch the cafual fparks of ire,

Like oil it kindles into mounting fire ;

And fiercely now his flaming fpirit blaz'd,

While on thofe galling words he wildly gaz'd,

Whofe force had almoft work'd into a ftorm

The gentler elements in beauty's form.

As

As the farcaftic fentence caught his view,

Back from the board his elbow-chair he drew,

And, by fharp ftings of fudden fury prick'd,

Far from his foot his gouty ftool he kick'd.

, Fierce as Achilles, by Atrides ftung,

He pour'd the ftream of vengeance from his tongue.

But ah, thofe angry threats he deign'd to fpeak,

Had founds, alas ! far differing from the Greek.

Rage from his lips in legal language broke ;

Of juries and of damages he fpoke,

And on the printer's law-devoted head

, He threaten'd deep revenge in terms moft dread ;

Terms, that with pain the ear of beauty pierce,

And oaths too rough to harmonize in verfe.

While thus the good old knight, with paffion hot,

His toaft neglected, and his tea forgot,

The difcord of the drama to increafe,

• Now prim PENELOPE affails her niece ;

For, as SIR GILBERT now, with choler dumb,

Points her the period with his angry thumb,

" Ah !

. " Ah ! brother," cries the stiff, malignant crone,
(Her sharp eye swiftly thro' the sentence thrown)
" Scandal could never rise to heights like this,
But from the manners of each modern miss ;
Had but my niece, less giddy and more grave,
Observ'd the prudent hints I often gave —— "
The honest knight her vile conclusion saw,
And quick curtail'd it with a testy " Pshaw !"
Mean while the gentle maid, who heard the taunt,
Survey'd without a frown her prudish aunt :
Far other thoughts employ'd her softer mind,
To one sweet purpose all her soul inclin'd ;
How she might close th' unpleasant scene, how best
Restore good-humour to her father's breast.
Her airy guardian with delight survey'd
These tender wishes in the lovely maid,
And, to accomplish what her heart desir'd,
Trains of new thought above her age inspir'd.
As Venus on her son's enlighten'd face
Shed richer charms, and more attractive grace,
                                        When,

When, iffuing forth from the diffolving cloud,

His bright form burft on the admiring crowd:

So kind SOPHROSYNE, unfeen, fupplies

A livelier radiance to SERENA's eyes;

And, ere fhe fpeaks, to captivate her fire,

Touches her lips with patriotic fire.

   It chanc'd, that, tofs'd upon a vacant chair,

A volume of that wit lay near the fair,

Whofe value, try'd by fafhion's varying touch,

Once rofe too high, and now is funk too much;

The book, which fortune plac'd within her reach,

Contain'd, O CHESTERFIELD, the liberal fpeech

In which thy fpirit, like an Attic fage,

Strove to defend the violated ftage

From fetters bafely forg'd by minifterial rage.

From this the nymph her ufeful leffon took,

And thus began, reclining on the book :—

" If on this noble lord we may rely,

Scandal is but a fpeck on Freedom's eye;

And.

And public fpirit, then, will rather bear
The cafual pain it gives by growing there,
Than, by a rafh attempt to move it thence,
Hazard the fafety of a precious fenfe,
And, by the efforts of a vain defire,
. Rob this life-darting eye of all its fire.
Tho' the foft breaft of innocence may fmart,
By cruel calumny's corroding dart,
Yet would fhe rather ache in every nerve,
And bear thofe pangs fhe knows not to deferve,
Much rather than be made a fenfelefs tool,
To aid the frenzy of tyrannic rule,
Or forge one dangerous bolt for power to aim
At facred Liberty's fuperior frame."——

As ancient chiefs were wont of old to gaze,
With eyes of tender awe and fond amaze
On the fair prieftefs of the Delphic fane,
When firft fhe utter'd her prophetic ftrain,
Entranc'd in wonder, thus SIR GILBERT view'd
His child, yet more infpir'd, who thus purfu'd:

" For

" For me, I own, thefe lines, with gall replete,

Shot thro' my fimple heart a fudden heat ;

But happier thoughts my rifing rage repreft,

And turn'd the pointlefs infult to a jeft :

And O ! fhould Slander ftill new wrath awake,

Still may my father, for his daughter's fake,

Difdain the vengeance of litigious ftrife,

And let SERENA's anfwer be—her life !"

She ended with a fmile, whofe magic flame

Shot youthful vigour thro' her father's frame :

His age, his anger, and his gout, are fled ;

" Enchanting girl !" with tears of joy, he faid,

" Enchanting girl !" twice echoed from his tongue,

As, fpeaking, from his elbow-chair he fprung,

" Come to thy father's arms !—By Heaven, thou art

His own true offspring, and a Whig in heart."

He fpoke ; and his fond arms around her curl'd

. With proud grafp, feeming to infold the world.

Her confcious heart fhe feels with triumph beat,

And joys to find that triumph is compleat ;

H   For

• For ftiff PENELOPE, who near them ftood,

. " Albeit unufed to the melting mood,"

Squeez'd from her eye-lid one reluctant tear,

And foften'd with a fmile her brow fevere ;

But 'twas a fmile of fuch a gloomy grace,

As lighten'd once upon Alecto's face,

When Orpheus paft her, leading back to life,

From Pluto's regions, his recover'd wife,

When love connubial, join'd to mufic's fpell,

Moiften'd with tender joy the eyes of hell.

Far other fmiles, with pleafure's fofteft air,

Gild the gay features of the youthful fair :

She looks like fportive Spring, when her young
     charms

Wind round her hoary fire's reluctant arms,

• And, by a frolic infantine embrace,

Banifh the rugged frown from Winter's face.

  Thro' the long day fhe felt the glowing tide

Of exultation thro' her bofom glide ;

And oft fhe wifh'd for flow-approaching night,

To hold fweet converfe with her guardian fprite.

At

At length the hour approach'd her heart defir'd,

And, in her lonely chamber now retir'd,

Her tender fancy gave the fondeft fcope

To ardent gratitude and eager hope.

" Dear airy being !" (the foft nymph exclaim'd)

" Whofe power can break the fpell that Spleen has
    fram'd,

Can, by the waving of thy viewlefs wing,

O'er darkeft forms a golden radiance fling,

And make, in minds by forrieft thoughts perplext,

This moment's grief the triumph of the next ;

I blefs thy fuccour in each trial paft ;

Be prefent ftill, and fave me in the laft !"

Thus, with her lovely eyes devoutly fixt,

Where rays of hope, and fear, and reverence mixt,

The tender fair her faithful guard addreft,

Then with her cheek her downy pillow preft ;

But long her wakeful lids refufe to clofe,

For curiofity difpels repofe.

Her bufy mind the myftic veil would pierce,

That hides the author of the pleafing verfe ;

H 2   Her

Her lips involuntary catch the chime,
And half articulate the foothing rhyme,
Till weary thought no longer watch can keep,
But finks reluctant in the folds of fleep.

END OF THE FOURTH CANTO.

CANTO

C A N T O   V.

WHY art thou fled, O bleft poetic time,
When Fancy wrought the miracles of rhyme;
When, darting from her ftar-encircled throne,
Her poet's eye commanded worlds unknown;
When, by her fiat made a mimic god,
He faw exiftence waiting on his nod,
And at his pleafure into being brought
New fhadowy hofts, the vaffals of his thought,
In joy's gay garb, in terror's dread array,
Darker than night, and brighter than the day;
Who, at his bidding, thro' the wilds of air,
Rais'd willing mortals far from earthly care,
And led them wondering thro' his wide domain,
Beyond the bounds of nature's narrow reign;
While their rapt fpirits, in the various flight,
Shook with fucceffive thrills of new delight?

Return, fweet feafon, grac'd with fiction's flowers,

Let not cold fyftem cramp thy genial powers !

Shall mild Morality, in garb uncouth,

The houfewife garb of plain and homely truth,

Robb'd by ftern Method of her rofy crown,

Chill her faint votaries by a wintry frown ?

No ; thou fweet friend of man, as fuits thee beft,

Shine forth in Fable's rich-embroider'd veft !

O make my verfe thy vehicle, thy arms,

To fpread o'er focial life thy potent charms !

And thou, SOPHROSYNE, myfterious fprite !

If haply I may trace thy fteps aright,

Roving thro' paths untrod by mortal feet,

To paint for human eyes thy heavenly feat,

Shed on my foul fome portion of that power,

Which fav'd SERENA in the trying hour,

To bear thofe trials, which, however hard,

As bards all tell us, may befall the bard ;

. The fop's pert jeft, the critic's frown fevere,

Learning's proud cant, with envy's artful fneer,

                                        And,

And, the vext poet's laſt and worſt diſgrace,

, His cold blank bookſeller's rhyme-freezing face.

Hence ! ye dark omens, that to Spleen belong,

Ye ſhall not check the current of my ſong,

While Beauty's lovely race, for whom I ſing,

Fire my warm hand to ſtrike the ready ſtring.

As quiet now her lighteſt mantle laid

O'er the ſtill ſenſes of the ſleeping maid,

Her nightly viſitant, her faithful guide,

. Deſcends in all her empyrean pride ;

That fairy ſhape no more ſhe deigns to wear,

Whoſe light foot ſmooths the furrow plough'd by care

In mortal faces, while her tiny ſpear

Gives a kind tingle to the caution'd ear.

Now, in her nobler ſhape, of heavenly ſize,

She ſtrikes her votary's ſoul with new ſurpriſe.

Jove's favourite daughter, arm'd in all his powers,

Appear'd leſs brilliant to th' attending Hours,

When, on the golden car of Juno rais'd,

In heavenly pomp the queen of battles blaz'd :

H 4   With

With all her luftre, but without the dread
Which from her arm the frowning gorgon fhed,
SOPHROSYNE defcends, with guardian love,
To waft her gentle ward to worlds above.
From her fair brow a radiant diadem
Rofe in twelve ftars, and every feparate gem
Shot magic rays, of virtue to controul
. Some paffion hoftile to the human foul.
Round her fweet form a robe of æther flow'd,
And in a wonderous car the fmiling Spirit rode;
. Firm as pure ivory, it charm'd the fight
With finer polifh and a fofter white.
The hand of beauty, with an eafy fwell,
Scoop'd the free concave like a bending fhell;
And on its rich exterior, art difplay'd
The triumphs of the Power the car convey'd.
Here, in celeftial tints, furpaffing life,
Sate lovely Gentlenefs, difarming Strife;
. There, young Affeftion, born of tender Thought,
In rofy chains the fiercer paffions caught;

                                          Ambition,

Ambition, with his fceptre fnapt in twain,

And Avarice, fcorning what his chefts contain.

Round the tame vulture flies the fearlefs dove;

Soft Innocence embraces playful Love;

And laughing Sport, the frolic child of Air,

Buries in flowers the finking form of Care.

    Thefe figures, pencil'd with a touch fo light,

That every image feem'd an heavenly fprite,

Breathe on the car; whofe fight-enchanting frame

Four wheels fuftain, of pale and purple flame;

For no fleet animals, to earth unknown,

Bear thro' ætherial fields this flying throne.

As by the fubtle electrician's fkill,

Globes feem to fly, obedient to his will;

So thefe four circles of inftinctive fire

Move by the impulfe of their queen's defire,

Mount or defcend by her directing care,

Or reft, fupported by the buoyant air.

    Now, fpringing from her car, that hovering ftaid

High in the chamber of the fleeping maid,

The

The goddefs, with a voice divinely clear,

Breath'd thefe kind accents in her votary's ear :—

" Come, my fair champion, who fo well haft fought

.The ufeful battles of contentious thought ;

To aid thy gentle fpirit to fuftain

The final conflict of thy deftin'd pain,

View the rewards that, in my realms of blifs,

Wait the fweet victor in fuch war as this !

So haply may thy mind, with ftrength renew'd,

The dark devices of the fiend elude ;

By one bleft effort feal thy triumphs paft,

.   And gain thy promis'd guerdon in the laft."

    As thus fhe fpake, her heavenly arms embrac'd,

And in the car the confcious maiden plac'd.

Quick at her wifh the flaming wheels afcend,

No clouds impede them, wherefoe'er they bend.

As thro' the empire of the winds they rufh'd,

The winds were all in mute fubmiffion hufh'd :

And now SERENA, from th' exalted car,

Look'd down, aftonifh'd, on each finking ftar ;

Flying

Flying o'er lucid orbs, whofe diftant light

Yet has not reach'd the fcope of human fight;

And now, not diftant from the bounds of fpace,

The guardian fprite fufpends their rapid race;

And, while in deep amaze the nymph admires

The circling meteors' inoffenfive fires,

Pleas'd at her wonder, the mild power addreft,

With kind intelligence, her earthly gueft :—

" Of thofe three orbs, that in yon cryftal fphere

A feparate fyftem in themfelves appear,

The laft, whofe luminous and fteady form

Shines foftly bright, and moderately warm,

Contains my palace, and the gentle train

Whom I have wafted to this pure domain.

At equal diftance my dominions lie

From thefe two larger worlds, more near thine eye :

Obferve their difference as our wheels advance,

And paffing, take of each a tranfient glance."

So fpeaking, to the groffer globe fhe fprung,

Her car fufpended o'er its furface hung,

In

In heavy air ; for round this orb was roll'd
A circling vapour, dull, and damp, and cold.
" Here," fays SOPHROSYNE, " thofe beings dwell,
• Who wanted foul to act or ill or well ;
Who faunter'd thoughtlefs thro' their mortal time,
Without a care, a virtue, or a crime ;
Here ftill they faunter, in this languid fcene :
But pafs the dozing crowd, and mark their queen."
And now, flow riding on a tortoife' back,
Her features lifelefs, and each fibre flack,
Full in their view the nymph Indifference came ;
The quick SERENA foon perceiv'd her name ;
For, as in folemn creeping ftate fhe rode,
In her lax hand fhe held fair GREVILLE's ode.
Ne'er did the mufe from her fweet treafure cull
Incenfe fo precious for a Power fo dull.
Still, as fhe mov'd along her even way,
The heavy goddefs try'd to read the lay ;
But at each paufe her inattentive eye
Stray'd from the paper, which fhe held awry ;

                                        Nor

Nor could her lips a fingle line repeat,

Tho' the foft verfe, moft ravifhingly fweet,

Thro' Time's juft ear will lafting pleafure fpread,

. And charm the poppy from Oblivion's head.

Thus, like a city mayor, whofe heavy barge

Steers its dull progrefs at the public charge,

This Power, fo cumber'd by her empire's weight,

Makes her flow circuit round her fluggifh ftate.

Around her, tribes of rambling fceptics crawl,

. Tho' moving, dubious if they move at all.

Before her, languid Pomp, her marfhal, creeps,

Whofe hand her banner half unfolded keeps:

Its quaint device her dull dominion fpoke—

. An eagle, numb'd by the torpedo's ftroke.

" Enough of fcenes fo foreign to thy foul,"

Sophrosyne exclaim'd; "/from this dark goal

Pafs we to regions oppofite to this."

She fpoke; and, darting o'er the wide abyfs;

Her car, like lightning in foft flafhes hurl'd,

Shot to the confines of a clearer world.

Now

Now lovelier views the virgin's mind abforb;

For now they hover'd o'er a lucid orb.

Here the foft air, luxuriantly warm,

Imparts new luftre to Serena's form:

Her eyes with more expreffive radiance fpeak,

And richer rofes open on her cheek.

Here, as fhe gaz'd, fhe felt in every vein

A blended thrill of pleafure and of pain;

Yet every object glittering in her view,

Her quick regard with foft attraction drew.

Sophrosyne, who faw the gentle fair

Lean o'er thefe confines with peculiar care,

Smil'd at the tender intereft fhe difplay'd,

And fpoke regardful of the penfive maid:

" Well may'ft thou bend o'er this congenial fphere;

For Senfibility is fovereign here.

Thou feeft her train of fprightly damfels fport,

Where the foft fpirit holds her rural court;

But fix thine eye attentive to the plain,

And mark the varying wonders of her reign."

As

As thus she spoke, she pois'd her airy seat
High o'er a plain exhaling every sweet;
For round its precincts all the flowers that bloom
Fill'd the delicious air with rich perfume;
And in the midst a verdant throne appear'd,
In simplest form by graceful fancy rear'd,
And deck'd with flowers; not such whose flaunting
    dyes
Strike with the strongest tint our dazzled eyes;
But those wild herbs that tenderest fibres bear,
And shun th' approaches of a damper air.
Here stood the lovely ruler of the scene,
And beauty, more than pomp, announc'd the queen.
The bending snow-drop, and the briar-rose,
The simple circle of her crown compose;
Roses of every hue her robe adorn,
Except th' insipid rose without a thorn.
Thro' her thin vest her heighten'd beauties shine;
For earthly gauze was never half so fine.
Of that enchanting age her figure seems,
When smiling nature with the vital beams

Of

Of vivid youth, and pleasure's purple flame,
Gilds her accomplish'd work, the female frame,
With rich luxuriance tender, sweetly wild,
And just between the woman and the child.
Her fair left arm around a vase she flings,
From which the tender plant mimosa springs:
Towards its leaves, o'er which she fondly bends,
The youthful fair her vacant hand extends
With gentle motion, anxious to survey
How far the feeling fibres own her sway:
The leaves, as conscious of their queen's command,
Successive fall at her approaching hand;
While her soft breast with pity seems to pant,
And shrinks at every shrinking of the plant.

　　Around their sovereign, on the verdant ground,
Sweet airy forms in mystic measures bound.
The mighty master of the revel, Love,
In notes more soothing than his mother's dove,
Prompts the soft strain that melting virgins sing,
Or sportive trips around the frolic ring,

Coupling,

Stothard del.   Neagle sculp.

Published as the Act directs by T. Cadell, Strand, Feb.ᵉʳ 1ˢᵗ 1788.

Coupling, with radiant wreaths of lambent fire,

Fair fluttering Hope and rapturous Defire.

Unnumber'd damfels different charms difplay,

Penfive with blifs, or in their pleafures gay ;

And the wide profpect yields one touching fight

Of tender, yet diverfified delight.

But, the bright triumphs of their joy to check,

In the clear air there hangs a dufky fpeck ;

It fwells—it fpreads—and rapid, as it grows,

O'er the gay fcene a chilling fhadow throws.

The foft SERENA, who beheld its flight,

Sufpects no evil from a cloud fo light ;

For harmlefs round her the thin vapours wreath,

Not hiding from her view the fcene beneath ;

But ah ! too foon, with pity's tender pain,

She faw its dire effect o'er all the plain :

Sudden from thence the founds of anguifh flow,

And joy's fweet carols end in fhrieks of woe :

The wither'd flowers are fall'n, that bloom'd fo fair,

And poifon all the peftilential air.

I

From

From the rent earth dark demons force their way,

And make the fportive revellers their prey.

Here gloomy Terror, with a fhadowy rope,

Seems, like a Turkifh mute, to ftrangle Hope;

There jealous Fury drowns in blood the fire

That fparkled in the eye of young Defire;

And lifelefs Love lets mercilefs Defpair

From his crufh'd frame his bleeding pinions tear.

But pangs more cruel, more intenfely keen,

Wound and diftract their fympathetic queen:

With fruitlefs tears fhe o'er their mifery bends;

From her fweet brow the thorny rofe fhe rends,

• And, bow'd by grief's infufferable weight,

Frantic fhe curfes her immortal ftate:

The foft SERENA, as this curfe fhe hears,

Feels her bright eye fuffus'd with kindred tears;

And her kind breaft, where quick compaffion fwell'd,

Shar'd in each bitter fuffering fhe beheld.

·The guardian Power furvey'd her lovely grief,

And fpoke in gentle terms of mild relief:

" For

" For this foft tribe thy heavieft fear difmifs,

, And know their pains are tranfient as their blifs :

. Rapture and agony, in nature's loom,

Have form'd the changing tiffue of their doom ;

Both interwoven with fo nice an art,

No power can tear the twifted threads apart :

Yet happier thefe, to Nature's heart more dear,

Than the dull offspring in the torpid fphere,

Where her warm wifhes, and affections kind,

Lofe their bright current in the ftagnant mind.

. Here grief and joy fo fuddenly unite,

That anguifh ferves to fublimate delight."

She fpoke ; and, ere SERENA could reply,

The vapour vanifh'd from the lucid fky ;

The nymphs revive, the fhadowy fiends are fled,

The new-born flowers a richer fragrance fhed ;

The gentle ruler of the changeful land,

Smiling, refum'd her fymbol of command ;

Replac'd the rofes of her regal wreath,

Still trembling at the thorns that lurk beneath:

But,

But, to her wounded fubjects quick to pay
The tender duties of imperial fway,
Their wants fhe fuccour'd, they her wifh obey'd,
And all recover'd, by alternate aid ;
While, on the lovely queen's enchanting face,
Departed forrow's faint and fainter trace,
. Gave to each touching charm a more attractive
    grace.
Now, laughing Sport, from the enlighten'd plain,
Clear'd with quick foot the veftiges of pain ;
The gay fcene grows more beautifully bright,
Than when it firft allur'd SERENA's fight,
Still her fond eyes o'er all the profpect range,
Flafhing fweet pleafure at the blifsful change :
Her curious thoughts with fond attachment burn,
Yet more of this engaging land to learn.
She finds the chief attendants of the queen,
Sweet females, wafted from our human fcene ;
But, as it chanc'd, while all the realm reviv'd,
A fpirit mafculine from earth arriv'd :

                           Two

Two airy guides conduct the gentle shade;
Genius, in robes of braided flames array'd,
And a fantastic nymph, in manners nice,
Profusely deck'd with many an odd device;
Sister of him, whose luminous attire
Flashes with unextinguishable fire;
Like him in features, in her look as wild,
And Singularity by mortals styl'd.
The eager queen, and all her smiling court,
Surround the welcome shade in gentle sport;
For in their new associate all rejoice,
All pant to hear the accents of his voice.
Tho' o'er his frame th' Armenian robe was flung,
The pleasing stranger spoke the Gallic tongue;
But in that language his enchanting art
Inspir'd new energy, that seiz'd the heart;
In terms so eloquent, so sweetly bold,
A story of disastrous love he told,
Convuls'd with sympathy, the list'ning train,
At every pause, with dear delicious pain,
Intreat him to renew the fascinating strain.

And

And now SERENA, with fufpended breath,

Liften'd, and caught the tale of Julia's death;

And quick fhe cries, ere tears had time to flow,

" Bleft be this hour! for now I fee Rouffeau."

Fondly fhe gaz'd, till the enchanting found

In fuch a potent fpell her fpirit bound,

That, loft in fweet illufion, fhe forgot

The promis'd fcenes of the fublimer fpot;

Till now her mild remembrancer, whofe care

Stray'd not a moment from the mortal fair,

Rous'd her rapt mind, preparing her to meet

The brighter wonders of her blifsful feat;

While her inftinctive car's obedient frame

, Now upward rofe, like undulating flame.

As when fome victor on the watery world,

Bright honour gilding all his fails unfurl'd,

Steers into port, while to the laughing fky

His ftreamers tell his triumph as they fly;

Expecting thoufands line the crowded ftrand,

Swell the glad voice, or wave the joyous hand,

Preffing

Preffing to view the fight their vows implor'd,   .

And hail their glory and their ftrength reftor'd:

So the bleft beings of this fmiling fcene   ·

Flock'd round the car of their returning queen.

The radiant car, from which they now alight,

Careful fhe gives to a felected fprite,

A nymph of fnowy veft and lovely frame,

Fidelity her fair and fpotlefs name;

Then, happy to review her hallow'd home,

Leads her fweet gueft to her celeftial dome.

    Gentleft of powers! for every purpofe fit,

.To ftrengthen wifdom, and embellifh wit;—

Thou, whofe foft arts, poffefs'd by thee alone,

.Can give to virtue's voice a fweeter tone;

Allay the froft of age, or fire of youth,

And lend attraction to fevereft truth;

Improve e'en beauty by thy graceful eafe,

Or teach deformity herfelf to pleafe;—

Infpire the bard, whofe juft ambition pants

To guide weak mortals to thy heavenly haunts!

                I 4   Grant

Grant him, in notes that, like thy foft controul,

Allure attention, and poffefs the foul ;

Grant him to fhow, in luminous difplay,

The myftic wonders of thy fecret fway !

Now, at the fight of the prefiding power,

Wide fpread the gates of a ftupendous tower,

On whofe firm height, commanding nature's bound,

The faithful warder of the fort they found,

Wakeful Intelligence, a trufty fprite,

Whofe eyes are piercing as the folar light,

And ever on the watch to found alarm,

If aught of dufky hue, portending harm,

Should, in defiance of her mandate, dare

Approach the palace of th' imperial fair.

Within his ward, magnificently great,

Lies the rich armoury that guards her ftate.

Here ftands Conviction's ftrong and lucid fpear,

Whofe touch annihilates fufpence and fear ;

Here, Truth's unfullied adamantine fhield,

Which, fave SOPHROSYNE, no power can wield ;

And

And Reafon's trenchant blade of blazing fteel,

Its edge and polifh form'd by friendly zeal;

And, not lefs fure their deftin'd mark to hit,

Pointed by virtue's hand, the fhafts of Wit;

And Ridicule's ftrong bolt, whofe ftunning blow

Lays towering vice and fearlefs folly low.

Here too the goddefs kept, in myftic ftate,

Thofe fweet rewards that on her champions wait,

Guerdons more precious than triumphant palms:—

The glance of gratitude for mental alms,

Peace's foft kifs, and reconcilement's tear,

And fmiles of fympathy, are treafur'd here.

 Thefe precincts paft, now hand in hand they came

To the rich fabric of majeftic frame;

Inftinct with joy their fovereign to behold,

The gates of maffive adamant unfold;

And, as the gently-moving valves unclofe,

Myfterious mufic from their motion flows;

The airy notes thro' all the palace roam,

.And dulcet echoes fill the feftive dome:

      A gorgeous

A gorgeous hall amaz'd Serena's eyes,

Compar'd to which, in fplendor, ftrength, and fize,

The nobleft works of which tradition fings,

Judaic fhrine, or feat of Memphian kings,

Would feem more humble than the waxen cell

In which the fkilful bee is proud to dwell.

. Here fits a power, in whofe angelic face

Beauty is fweeten'd by maternal grace;

Her radiant feat, furpaffing mortal art,

Supports an emblem of her liberal heart,

A pelican, who rears her callow brood,

And from her vitals feems to draw their food.

Around this fpirit flock a filial hoft,

Who blefs her empire, and her guidance boaft.

Here every fcience, all the arts attend,

In her they hail their parent and their friend;

Each to her prefence brings the happy few,

Whofe deareft glory from her favour grew.   .

Here, in her fimple charms, with youthful fire,

Proud to difplay the magic of her lyre,

Soul-

Soul-foothing Harmony prefents her band :

Befide her Orpheus and Amphion ftand.

Here, mild Philofophy, whofe thoughtful frown

Is fweetly fhaded by her olive crown,

(In all her Attic elegance array'd,

. Strong to convince, and gentle to perfuade)

To her, whofe breath infpir'd his every rule,

Leads the bleft fire of the Socratic fchool.

Each animating bard and moral fage,

The heaven-taught minds of every clime and age,

Who foften'd manners, and refin'd the foul,

Flock to this prefence, as to glory's goal ;

And, as the mother's heart, that yearns to blefs

The rival innocents that round her prefs,

Delights to fee them, as her love they fhare,

Sport in her fight, and flourifh by her care ;

Fondly refponfive to their every call,

. Tender of each, and provident for all :

So this fweet image of celeftial grace,

Who fits encircled by her lovely race,

To

To every fcience vital ftrength imparts,

And rears the circle of the focial arts ;

With fuch folicitude fhe gives to each,

Pow'rs of fublimer aim and wider reach.

And now Sophrosyne, who near her preft,

Thus fpoke her title to her earthly gueft :—

" Behold the honour'd form, without whofe aid

My ftrength muft vanifh, and my glory fade !

Source of my being, and my life's fupport !

Eunoia call'd in this celeftial court,

Benevolence the name fhe bears on earth,

The guard of weaknefs, and the friend of worth."

　　She ended: and the mild maternal form

Embrac'd Serena with a fmile as warm

As the gay fpirit Vegetation wears,

When fhe to crown her favourite nymph prepares,

When, pleas'd her flowery treafures to difplay,

She pours them in the lap of youthful May.

　　But how, Serena ! how may human fpeech

Thy heavenly raptures in this moment reach ?

　　　　　　　　　　　　　　　　　If

If aught of earthly fentiment may vie

With the pure joy thefe happy fcenes fupply,

'Tis when, unmixt with trouble and with pain,

Love glides in fecret thro' the glowing vein ;

When fome fond youth, unconfcious of its fire,

Free from chill fear and turbulent defire,

With every thought abforb'd in foft delight,

Sees all creation in his fair one's fight,

And feels a blifsful ftate without a name,

Repofe of foul with harmony of frame.

So, plung'd in pleafure of the pureft kind,

SERENA gaz'd on the maternal mind ;

Gaz'd till SOPHROSYNE's directing aid

Thus fummon'd to new fights th' obedient maid:—

" Hafte, my fair charge, for of this ample ftate,

Tracts yet unfeen thy vifitation wait.

The prefling hours forbid me to unfold

Each feparate province which thefe confines hold ;

But I will lead thee to that blifsful crew,

Whofe kindred fpirits beft deferve thy view."

So

So fpeaking, her attentive gueft fhe led
Thro' fcenes, that ftill increafing wonder bred.
Where'er fhe trod, thro' all her gorgeous feat,
Soft mufic echoed from beneath her feet :
Paffing a portal, on whofe lucid ftone
Emblems of innocence and beauty fhone,
They reach a lawn with verdant luftre bright,
And view the bowers of permanent delight.
No fiery fun here forms a fcorching noon,
No baleful meteor gleams, no chilling moon :
But, from a latent fource, one foothing light,
Whofe conftant rays repel the mift of night,
Tho' tender, chearful, and tho' warm, ferene,
Gives lafting beauty to the lovely fcene.
No fenfual thought this paradife profanes ;
• For here tried excellence in triumph reigns,
Benignant cares eternal joy fupply,
And blifs angelic beams in every eye.
    " In yonder groups," the leading fpirit cried,
" My fav'rite females fee, my faireft pride.

                                    The

The firſt in rank is that diſtinguiſh'd train,

Whoſe ſtrength of ſoul was tried by Hymen's chain :

Tho' beauty bleſt their form, and love, their guide,

Their nuptial band with happieſt omens tied,

Beauty and love, they felt, may loſe the art

To fix inconſtant man's eccentric heart ;

Yet, conſcious of their lord's neglected vow,

No virtue frown'd outrageous on their brow,

To keep returning tenderneſs aloof,

By coarſe upbraiding, and deſpis'd reproof :

With ſorrow ſmother'd in attraction's ſmile,

They ſtrove the ſenſe of miſery to beguile ;

And, from wild paſſion's perilous abyſs,

Lure the loſt wanderer back to faithful bliſs.

See mild Octavia o'er this band preſide,

Voluptuous Antony's neglected bride,

Whoſe feeling heart, with all a mother's care,

Rear'd the young offspring of a rival fair.

Far other trials rais'd yon lovely crew,

Tho' in connubial ſcenes their merit grew :

It

It was their chance, ere judgment was mature,

When glittering toys the infant mind allure,

Following their parents' avaricious rule,

To wed, with hopes of blifs, a wealthy fool.

When time remov'd delufion's veil by ftealth,

And fhow'd the drear vacuity of wealth ;

When fad experience prov'd the bitter fate

Of beauty coupled to a fenfelefs mate,

Thefe gentle wives ftill gloried to fubmit ;

Thefe, tho' invited by alluring wit,

Refus'd in paths of lawlefs joy to range,

Nor murmur'd at the lot they could not change :

But, with a lively fweetnefs, unoppreft

By a dull hufband's lamentable jeft,

Their conftant rays of gay good-humour fpread

A guardian glory round their idiot's head.

The next in order are thofe lovely forms,

Whofe patience weather'd all paternal ftorms ;

By filial cares, the mind's unfailing teft,

Well have they earn'd thefe feats of blifsful reft :

They,

They, unrepining at fevere reftraint,

Peevifh commands, and undeferv'd complaint;

Bent with unwearied kindnefs to appeafe

Each fancied want of querulous difeafe;

Gave up thofe joys which youthful hearts engage,

To watch the weaknefs of parental age.

Turn to this chearful band; and mark in this,

Spirits who juftly claim my realms of blifs!

Moft lovely thefe! when judg'd by generous truth,

Tho' beauty is not their's, nor blooming youth:

For thefe are they, who, in life's thorny fhade,

Repin'd not at the name of ancient maid.

No proud difdain, no narrownefs of heart,

Held them from Hymen's tempting rites apart;

But fair difcretion led them to withdraw

From the priz'd honour of his proffer'd law;

To quit the object of no hafty choice,

In mild fubmiffion to a parent's voice;

The valued lover with a figh refign,

And facrifice delight at duty's fhrine.

K   With

With fmiles they bore, from angry fpleen exempt,
Injurious mockery, and coarfe contempt :
'Twas their's to clafp, each felfifh care above,
A fifter's orphans with parental love,
And all her tender offices fupply,
Tho' bound not by the ftrong maternal tie :
'Twas their's to bid inteftine quarrels ceafe,
And form the cement of domeftic peace.
No throbbing joy their fpotlefs bofom fir'd,
Save what benevolence herfelf infpir'd ;
No praife they fought, except that praife refin'd,
Which the heart whifpers to the worthy mind.
    Such are thefe gentle tribes, the happy few
Who fhare the triumph to their victory due :
Angelic aims their fpotlefs minds employ,
And fill their meafure of unchequer'd joy.
Behold ! where fome with generous ardour wait
Around yon feer, who holds the book of fate ;
Thofe awful leaves with eager glance they turn,
Thence with celeftial zeal they fondly learn

                                        What

What dangers threaten, thro' the vale of earth,

Their kindred pilgrims, ere they rife to birth:

To earth they ftill invifibly defcend,

In that dark fcene congenial minds defend,

From pleafure's bud drive fpleen's corroding worm,

And in my votaries' heart my power confirm.

   Delights more calm yon liftening band employ,

Who deeply drink of intellectual joy.

See them around that fpeaking nymph rejoice,

Their pleafures varying with her varied voice !

What graces in the fweet enthufiaft glow !

Repeating here whate'er fhe learns below.

Memory her name, her charge o'er earth to flit,

And cull the faireft flowers of human wit.

Whatever Genius, in his happieft hour,

Has penn'd, of moral grace and comic power,

To warm the heart, the fpells of Spleen unbind,

And pour gay funfhine o'er the mifty mind;

Teach men to cherifh their fraternal tie,

And view kind nature with a filial eye;

This

This active spirit catches in her flight,
Skill'd to retain, and happy to recite.
Here she delivers each bright work, and each
. Derives new beauty from her graceful speech.
Warpt by no envy, by no love misled,
Equal she holds the living and the dead ;
Alike rehearsing, as they claim their turn,
The song of Anstey, and the tale of Sterne.

But morning calls thee hence.—Yet one scene
    more,
My fostering love shall lead thee to explore.
This, thy last fight, with careful eyes survey,
And mark th' extensive nature of my sway."

Thus with fond zeal the guardian Spirit said,
And to new precincts of her palace led ;
The scene she enter'd of her richest state,
Where on her voice the subject passions wait :
Here rose a throne of living gems, so bright
No breath could fully their benignant light ;
This, her immortal seat, the gracious guide
Assum'd : her ward stood wondering at her side.

.Swift

Swift as they felt their ruling Power inthron'd,

Ætherial beings, who her empire own'd,

Crowded in glittering pomp the gorgeous fcene,

To pay their homage to their heavenly queen.

    Firft came chafte Love, whofe fweet harmonious
       form

Ne'er felt fufpicion's foul-convulfing ftorm ;

No baleful arrow in his quiver lies,

No blinding veil inwraps his fparkling eyes ;

There all the rays of varied joy unite,

And jointly fhed unfpeakable delight.

With him was Friendfhip, like a virgin dreft,

The foft afbeftos form'd her fimple veft,

Whofe wond'rous folds, in fierceft flames entire,

Mock the vain ravage of confuming fire :

Around this robe, a myftic chain fhe wore,

Each golden link a ftar of diamonds bore ;

Force could not tear the finifh'd work apart,

Nor int'reft loofe it by his fubtleft art :

But, ftrange to tell, if the prefiding Power,

Who to her favourite gave this precious dower,

If

If kind SOPHROSYNE could fail to breathe
Her vital virtue on this magic wreath,
The parts muſt ſever, faithleſs to their truſt,
The gold grow droſs, and every diamond duſt.
Theſe Valour follow'd, deck'd with verdant palm,
Gracefully bold, majeſtically calm.
A mingled troop ſucceed, with feſtive ſound,
.Wiſdom with olive, Wit with feathers crown'd ;
Here, hand in hand they move, no longer foes,
Their charms increaſing as their union grows ;
Pure ſpirits all, who hating mental ſtrife,
Exalt creation, and embelliſh life ;
All here attend, and, in their ſovereign's praiſe,
Their circling forms the ſong of glory raiſe.

    The bleſt SERENA drinks, with raviſh'd ear,
The melting muſic of the tuneful ſphere.
Now in its cloſe the ſoothing echoes roll
O'er her rapt fancy, and intrance her ſoul;
Her ſenſes ſink in ſoft oblivion's bands,
Till faithful Jenny at her pillow ſtands,

                                    Recalls

Recalls each mental and corporeal power,

While fhe proclaims aloud the paffing hour;

And, in a voice expreffive of furprife,

Too fhrill to feem the mufic of the fkies,

Informs the ftartled fair 'tis time to rife.

END OF THE FIFTH CANTO.

CANTO VI.

BLEST be the heart of fympathetic mould,
Whatever form that gentle heart infold,
Whofe generous fibres with fond terror fhake,
When keen affliction threatens to o'ertake
Young artlefs beauty, as alarm'd fhe ftrays
Thro' the ftrange windings of this mortal maze!
To fuch, SERENA, be thy ftory known,
Whofe bofom beft can make thy lot their own,
And, kindly fharing in thy trials paft,
Attend with fweet anxiety the laft.
The hour approaches, the tremendous hour,
In whofe dark moments deeper perils lower;
Still fo inwrapt in pleafure's gay difguife,
They lurk invifible to caution's eyes;
And, unfufpected by the fair one, wait
To cancel or confirm her blifsful fate.

                                        Her

Her lively mind with bright ideas ſtor'd,
She takes her ſtation at the breakfaſt-board;
Still her ſoft ſoul the heavenly viſion fills,
And ſweeter graces in her ſmile inſtils;
New hopes of triumph glide thro' every nerve,
And arm her glowing heart with firm reſerve;
Conſcious the final trying chance impends,
To bear its force her every power ſhe bends;
In her quick thought ambitious to preſage
How Spleen's dark agents may exert their rage,
She ponders on what perils may befall,
And fondly deems her mind a match for all.
Ah, lovely nymph! this dangerous pride forego;
Pride may betray—ſecurity's thy foe.

    While fancied prudence thus, a foreign gueſt,
Sits doubly cheriſh'd in SERENA's breaſt,
Behold a billet her attention ſteal,
No common arms compoſe its ample ſeal;
Th' unfolding paper breathes a roſeate ſcent,
Sweet harbinger of joy, its kind intent.

Of

Of courteous FILLIGREE it bears the name,

Clear fymptom of the peer's increafing flame !

The gracious earl, lamenting pleafure loft,

And fair SERENA in her wifhes croft,

Has plann'd, in honour of the lovely maid,

A fancied ball, a private mafquerade,

And fupplicates her fire, with warm efteem,

To fmile indulgent on the feftive fcheme.

All arts he ufes to infure the grant,

Nor leaves unafk'd the eager maiden aunt.

Quick at the found SERENA's glowing heart

Throbs with gay hopes ; but foon thofe hopes depart :

Reflection, in her foul a faithful guard,

The opening avenues of pleafure barr'd :

She deem'd the plan of this delightful fhow,

But the new ambufh of her fecret foe ;

The blifs too bright to realize, fhe guefs'd,

And chas'd th' idea from her guarded breaft.

While thefe difcreet refolves her thought employ,

Tranquil fhe triumphs o'er her fmother'd joy.

Not

Not fo the knight—to his parental eyes,
In dazzling pomp delufive vifions rife:
That coronet, the object of his vow,
He fees fufpended o'er his daughter's brow;
. Eager he burns to fnap the pendent thread,
And fix the glory on his darling's head.
Far wifer aims the ancient maiden taught,
No empty gew-gaw flutters in her thought;
But, while more keenly fhe applauds the plan,
. Her hope is folid and fubftantial man;
Not for her infant niece, whofe baby frame
She holds unfit for Hymen's holy flame;
But for her riper felf, whofe ftrength may bear
, The heavieft burden of connubial care.

    Tho' different phantoms dance before their fight,
• Niece, aunt, and father, in one wifh unite,
To join the banquet is their common choice,
• The bufinefs paft with no diffenting voice;
And the warm fire, in whom ambition burn'd,
A note of grateful courtefy return'd:

His billet feal'd, the glad good-humour'd knight

Launch'd forth, like Neftor, on his youthful
     might:—

" O could I now, in fpite of age, retain

That active vigour, and that fprightly vein,

Which led me once the lively laugh to raife

Among the merrier wits of former days,

When rival beauties would around me throng,

And gay ridottos liften to my fong !

Such were I now, as on the feftive night,

When Ch——h's charms amaz'd the public fight;

When the kind fair one, in a veil fo thin

That the clear gauze was but a lighter fkin,

Mafk'd like a virgin juft prepar'd to die,

Gave her plump beauties to each greedy eye !

On that fam'd night (for then with frolic fire

Youth fill'd my heart, and humour ftrung my lyre),

Pleas'd in the funfhine of her fmile to bafk,

I danc'd around her in a devil's mafk ;

And idly chanted an infernal ode,

In praife of all this female tempter fhow'd.

                                        The

The jocund crowd, who throng'd with me to gaze,

Extoll'd my unpremeditated lays,

And Sport, who ftill of this old revel brags,

* Styl'd her the firft of maids, and me of wags.

Then a light devil, now, reduc'd to limp,

I am but fit to play the hag-born imp ;

Still, not to crofs the frolic of this ball,

Still as the tortoife Caliban I'll crawl,

And if with gout my burning ankles flinch,

I'll call it Profpero's tormenting pinch ;

Still in this fhape I'll fhow them what I am :

And PEN. fhall go as Sycorax, my dam."

 So fpoke the knight ; and fpoke with fo much
   weight,

The liftening females faw his word was fate ;

For ne'er did Jove with fo refolv'd a brow

To fmiling Love his joyous fcheme avow,

* Θεων Δα, Νιϛορι τ'ανδρων.
   See Neftor's fpeech in the 11th Iliad.

       When

When be concerted, for his fpecial mirth,

A mafquerading on the ftage of earth,

And of the fwan's foft plume, or bull's rough hair,

Order'd the fancy-drefs he chofe to wear.

From whence let fapient antiquarians fhow

The ancient ufe of mafquerades below.

SERENA fmil'd to fee this joyous fire

Infufe new youth in her determin'd fire ;

But mute PENELOPE, with half a figh,

• " With one aufpicious and one dropping eye,"

Heard the firm knight his fixt refolve impart,

Tickling at once and torturing her heart.

The ball fhe relifh'd, but abhorr'd the tafk

To hide her beauties in a beldam's mafk :

Miranda's name would better fuit her plan,

A fimple maiden, not afraid of man ;

But us'd, alas ! her brother's law to feel,

She knows that law admits not of repeal.

Trufting her charms will any garb enrich,

She deigns to take the habit of a witch.

Never

Never did forcerefs in the fhades of night
Try to illuminate a filthy fprite
With fonder efforts, or with worfe fuccefs,
Than PEN. now labour'd, in this wayward drefs,
To give the fprightly fhow of living truth
To the poor ghoft of her departed youth.
As witches o'er their magic cauldron bend,
Anxious to fee their menial imps afcend;
So in her glafs the ancient maiden pries,
And dreams new graces in her perfon rife.
No fuch delights, whofe dear delufions pleafe,
The mild SERENA in her mirror fees;
She, at whofe toilet beauty's latent queen
Attends, enchanted with her filial mien,
And o'er her favourite's unconfcious face
Breathes her own rofeate glow and vivid grace.
She haftes her glittering garments to adjuft,
With all the modeft charms of fweet diftruft,
Doubting that beauty, which fhe doubts alone,
Which dazzles every eye except her own.

The

The native diffidence which fway'd her mind,

Now feels new terrors with its own combin'd;

The robes of Ariel to the nymph recall

Thofe difappointments that may yet befall;

As her fair hands the gauze or tiffue touch,

They fondly warn her not to hope too much.

She feels the friendly counfel they impart,

And caution reigns protector of her heart.

　　The fateful evening comes—the coach attends,

And firft the gouty Caliban afcends;

Then, in deformity's well-fuited pride,

, Sour Sycorax is ftation'd by his fide;

And laft, with fportive fmiles, divinely fweet,

Light Ariel perches on the vacant feat.

Fancy now paints the fcene of pleafure near,

, Yet fluttering gaiety is check'd by fear.

Her wifh to view the feftive fight runs high;

But the fond nymph remembers, with a figh,

. From hope's keen hand the cup of joy may flip,

And fall untafted, though it reach the lip.

　　　　　　　　　　　　　　　As

As the fine artist, whose nice toils aspire

To fame eternal by encaustic fire;

If he, with grief, has seen the faithless heat

Mar the rich labour it should make compleat,

When next his hands, with trembling care, confide

To the fierce element his pencil's pride,

Watches unceasing the pernicious flame,

Terror and hope contending in his frame,

While his fair work the dangerous fire sustains,

Feels it in all his sympathetic veins,

And at each trivial sound that chance may cause,

Hears the gem crack, and sees its cruel flaws:

With such solicitude the panting maid

Past the long street, of every noise afraid.

Now, while around her rival flambeaus flare,

And the coach rattles thro' the crowded square,

She fears some dire mischance must yet befall,

Some demon snatch her from the promis'd ball;

And dreams no trial more severe than this,

So bright she figures the new scene of bliss:

Yet,

Yet, horrid as it feems, her heart is bent
· To bear e'en this, and bear it with content.

But, whirl'd at length within the porter's gate,
She thinks what perils at the ball may wait ;
And, as fhe now alights, the fluttering fair
Invokes her guardian to protect her there,
Till thoughts of danger, thoughts of caution, fly
Before the magic blaze that meets her eye.
Th' advancing nymph, at every ftep fhe takes,
Pants with amazement, doubtful if fhe wakes ;
Far as her eyes the glittering fcene command,
'Tis all enchantment, all a fairy land ;
No veftiges of modern pomp appear,
No modern melody falutes her ear :
With Moorifh notes the echoing manfion rings,
And its tranfmuted form to fancy brings
The rich * Alhambra of the Moorifh kings.
The peer, who keenly thirfts for fafhion's praife,
To gild his revel with no common rays,

* See the views of this palace in Swinburn's Travels.

Summon'd

Summon'd his modiſh architeĉt, whoſe ſkill
Can all the wiſhes of caprice fulfil.
His genius, equal to the wildeſt taſk,
Gave to the houſe itſelf a Gothic maſk.
The chaplain, that no gueſt might feel negleĉt,
As a magician of the Arab ſeĉt,
Wav'd a preſiding wand throughout the ball,
And well provided for the wants of all.

The peer himſelf, his prowefs to evince,
Shines in the ſemblance of a Mooriſh prince;
And round the brilliant mimic hero wait
All pomp and circumſtance of Mooriſh ſtate:
Thro' all his ſplendid dome no eye could find
Aught unembelliſh'd, ſave the maſter's mind.
There, tho' repreſt by courteſy's controul,
Lurks the low mover of the little ſoul,
Mean vanity; whoſe ſlave can never prove
The heart-refining flame of genuine love.
While her cold joys his abjeĉt mind amuſe,
His thoughts are buſied on connubial views.

L 2   His.

His houfe compleat, its decorations plac'd
By the fure hand of fafhionable tafte,
He only wants, to crown his modifh life,
That laft and fineft moveable—a wife.
She too muft prove, to fix his coy defire,
Such as the eye of fafhion will admire.
His ball is but a jury, to decide
Upon the merit of his fancied bride.
If fweet SERENA, on this fignal night,
Shines the firft idol of the public fight;
If gallantry's fixt eyes pronounce her fair,
By the fure fign of one unceafing ftare;
And if, prophetic of her nobler doom,
Each rival beauty fhudders at her bloom;
The die is caft—he weds—the point is clear;
She cannot flight the vows of fuch a peer.
Thus argued in his mind the feftive earl,
And, left he lightly chufe an awkward girl,
Wifely conven'd, on this important cafe,
Each fafhionable judge of female grace.

Here

Here beaux efprits in various figures lurk,

Of Jew and Gentile, Bramin, Tartar, Turk;

But of the manly maſks, a youthful bard

Seem'd moſt to challenge beauty's ſoft regard:

Adorn'd with native elegance, he wore,

In ſimpleſt form, the minſtrel dreſs of yore:

They call him EDWIN, who around him throng,

EDWIN, immortaliz'd in Beattie's ſong;

And, ſooth to ſay, within a comely frame,

He bore a heart that anſwer'd to the name;

For this neat habit deck'd a generous youth,

Of gentleſt manners, and ſincereſt truth.

Tho' on his birth propitious fortune ſmil'd,

No proud parental folly ſpoil'd the child;

And genius, more beneficently kind,

Bleſt with ſuperior wealth his manly mind.

Of years he barely counted twenty-one;

But, like a brilliant morn, his opening life begun.

Fain would the muſe on this her votary dwell,

And fully paint the youth ſhe loves ſo well;

His

His figure's charms, the mufic of his tongue,
What nymphs his lays allur'd, what lays he fung:
But higher cares her rambling fong controul;
SERENA's perils fummon all her foul;
For Spleen, ambitious to exert her force,
Confcious this trial is her laft refource,
Moft keenly bent on her pernicious talk,
Has fhifted round the ball from malk to malk,
Watching the moment, with infernal care, ⎫
To form with deepeft art her final fnare, ⎬
And manacle the mind of the unguarded fair. ⎭

It comes, the moment that muft fix her lot,
By her, ah thoughtlefs maid! by her forgot;
Tho' the light Hours, e'en in their frolic ring,
Trembling perceive the fearful chance they bring,
And, fhuddering at the nymph's terrific ftate,
Seem anxious to fufpend her doubtful fate.

Now focial eafe the place of fport fupplied, ⎫
The hot oppreffive malk was thrown afide, ⎬
And beauty fhone reveal'd in all her blufhing pride. ⎭

Superior

Superior ſtill in features as in form,
With admiration fluſh'd, with pleaſure warm,
The gay SERENA every eye allur'd ;
, The hearts her figure won her face ſecur'd :
A tender ſweetneſs ſtill the nymph maintain'd,
, And modeſty o'er all her graces reign'd.
Well might her ſoul to brilliant hopes incline,
A thouſand youths had call'd her charms divine ;
A thouſand friends had whiſper'd in her ear,
That fate had mark'd her for the feſtive peer.
Her youthful fancy, tho' by pomp amus'd,
Wiſh'd not thoſe offers, which her heart refus'd :
That tender heart, by no vain pride poſſeſt,
With indeciſive trembling ſhook her breaſt,
Like a young bird, that, fluttering in the air,
Wiſhes to build her neſt, yet knows not where.

   The buſy earl, his puny love to raiſe,
Hunted the circling whiſper of her praiſe ;
Heard envy own her lovely charms, tho' loth,
Heard taſte atteſt them with a modiſh oath ;

And,

And, nuptial projects thickening in his mind,

Now his fair partner in the dance rejoin'd.

As now the fprightly mufic paus'd, my lord

Eager refolv'd to touch a fofter chord ;

Secure of all repulfe, he vainly meant

Half to difplay, half hide his fond intent,

And, in diffembled paffion's flowery tropes,

To fport at leifure with the virgin's hopes :

For this he fram'd a motley fpeech, replete

With amorous compliment and vain conceit.

The labour'd nothing with complacent pride

He fpoke ; but to his fpeech no nymph replied :

For in the moment, the loft fair devotes

Her willing ear to more attractive notes.

The minftrel happen'd near the nymph to walk,

Rapt with a bofom-friend in fecret talk,

And, at the inftant when the earl began

Half to unfold his matrimonial plan,

EDWIN, in whifpers, from the crowd retir'd,

Chanc'd to repeat the fonnet fhe infpir'd :

The

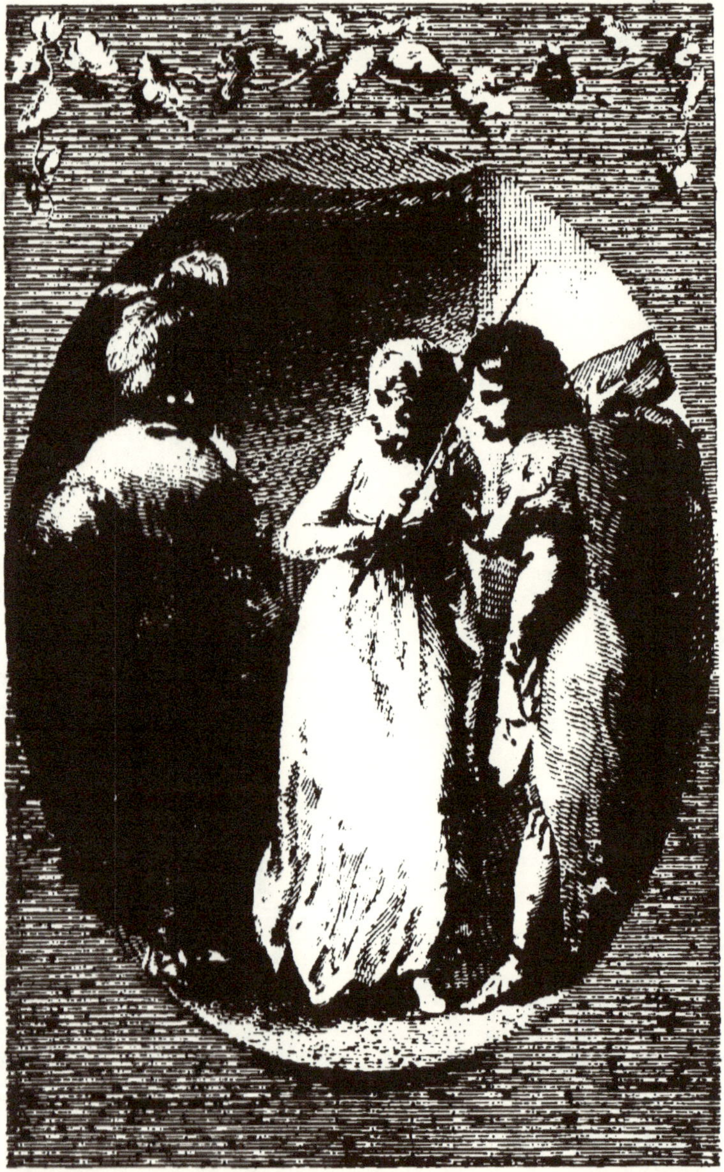

Stothard del.   Sharp sculp.

London,Publish'd Sept.r 1.st 1787, by T. Cadell, Strand.

The founds, tho' faint, her recollection caught,

Drew her quick eye, and fixt her wondering thought.

Loft in this fweet furprife, fhe could not hear

A fingle accent of the amorous peer.

Spleen faw the moment that fhe fought to gain,

And perch'd triumphant on the noble's brain.

With jealous envy ftung, and baffled pride,

" Contemptuous girl!" with fudden rage, he cried,

" If here to happier youths thy views incline,

I want not fairer nymphs who challenge mine.

Thy breaft in vain with penitence may burn;

But, once neglected, I no more return."

Thus loudly fpeaking, with diftemper'd heat,

Rudely he turn'd, with rancorous fcorn replete.

SERENA, ftartled at th' injurious found,

Survey'd th' infulting peer, who fternly frown'd;

Shame and refentment thro' her bofom rufh,

Swell every vein, and raife the burning blufh.

Love, new-born love, but in its birth conceal'd,

Nor to the nymph herfelf as yet reveal'd,

And

And juft difdain, and anger's honeft flame,

With complicated power convulfe her frame :

Contending paffions every thought confound,

And in tumultuous doubt her foul is drown'd.

Now treacherous pride, who tempts her tongue to trip,

Forms to a keen reply her quivering lip :

, Infidious Spleen now hovers o'er the fair,

Deems her half lock'd within her hateful fnare ;

In her new flave preparing to rejoice,

To taint her fpirit, and untune her voice.

Haplefs Serena ! what can fave thee now ?

The fiend's dark fignet ftamps thy clouded brow,

In thy fwoln eye I fee the ftarting drop ;

This fatal fhower, ætherial guardian ! ftop :

Hafte to thy votary, hafte, her foul fuftain,

, Nor let the trials fhe has paft be vain.

Ah me ! while yet I fpeak, with fhuddering dread

I hear the magic girdle's burfting thread.

This horrid omen, ye kind powers ! avert :

Nor thou, bright zone ! thy brighter charge defert.

Ah,

Ah, fruitlefs prayer! her panting breaft behold!

See! the gauze fhakes in many a ruffled fold!

Forc'd from their ftation by her heaving heart,

From the ftrain'd girdle thrice three fpangles ftart:

Thro' her diforder'd drefs a pafs they've found,

And fallen, fee, they glitter on the ground!—

.O blefled chance! with life-recalling light

The glittering monitors attract her fight!

Like ftars emerging from the darken'd pole,

They fparkle fafety to her harrafs'd foul.

See! from her brow the clouds of trouble fly,

Vexation's tear is vanifh'd from her eye!

. Her rofy cheeks with joy's foft radiance burn,

Like nature fmiling at the fun's return;

.The nymph, no more with mental darknefs blind,

Shines the fweet ruler of her refcu'd mind.

Hence, hateful Spleen! thy fancied prize refign,

Renounce for ever what fhall ne'er be thine;

For, confcious of her airy guardian's aid,

She feels new fpirit thro' her heart convey'd,

And,

And, inly bleffing this victorious hour,

Her foul exults in its recover'd power.

In fuch mild terms fhe hails th' infulting peer,

As Spleen, if mortal, muft expire to hear;

But, driven for ever from the lovely girl,

The foul fiend riots in the captive earl.

He anfwers not; but, with a fullen air,

On happier EDWIN, who approach'd the fair,

.Darts fuch a glance of rage and envious hate,

As Satan caft on Eden's blifsful ftate,

When on our parents firft he fixt his fight,

. And undelighted gaz'd on all delight:

So doom'd to look, and doom'd fuch pangs to feel,

. Scornful he turn'd on his elaftic heel.

" O lovely mildnefs! oh angelic maid!

Deferving homage, tho' to fcorn betray'd;

Rife ftill, fweet fpirit, rife thefe wrongs above,

Turn from injurious pride to faithful love;

Tho'

'Tho' on my brow no coronet may shine,

Wealth I can offer at thy beauty's shrine,

• And, worthier thee, a heart that worships thine."

Thus, with new-kindled love's aspiring flame,

Spoke the fond youth conceal'd by EDWIN's name,

The gallant FALKLAND, rich in inborn worth,

By fortune blest, and not of abject birth.

Warmly he spoke, with that indignant heat

With which the generous heart ne'er fails to beat,

• When worth insulted wakens virtuous ire,

And injur'd beauty sets the soul on fire.

Quick to his voice the startled virgin turn'd,

With wonder, hope, and joy, her bosom burn'd;

With sweet confusion, flurried and amaz'd,

On his attractive form she wildly gaz'd.

Full on her thought the friendly visions rush'd;

, Blushing she view'd him, view'd him still and
blush'd;

And, soft affection quickening at the sight,

Perchance had swoon'd with fullness of delight,

But

But that her father's voice, with quick controul,

Recall'd the functions of her fainting soul.

When on the diftant feat, where, fondly fixt,

He view'd the nymph as in the dance fhe mixt,

He indiftinctly heard, with wounded ear,

The fpleenful outrage of the angry peer,

Swift at th' imperfect found, with choler wild,

He fprung to fuccour his infulted child ;

But ere his fury into language broke,

Love calm'd the ftorm that arrogance awoke.

The fudden burft of FALKLAND's tender flame,

His winning manners, his diftinguifh'd name,

His liberal foul, by fortune's fmile careft,

All join'd to harmonize the father's breaft.

His fiery thoughts fubfide in glad furprife,

And to the generous youth he warmly cries :

" Ingenuous FALKLAND ! by thy franknefs won,

My willing heart would own thee as my fon ;

But on thy hopes SERENA muft decide :—

Hafte we together from this houfe of pride."

So

So fpoke the fire ; for, to her votary kind,

SOPHROSYNE infpir'd his foften'd mind.

Speaking, he fmil'd, to fee that on his word

The lover hung, and bleft the founds he heard ;

That his embarrafs'd child his fentence caught

With each tumultuous fign of tender thought ;

Whofe blufhes, fpringing from the heart, declare

The dawn of fondnefs in the modeft fair.

Th' enchanted youth with ecftafy convey'd

Forth from the troubled feaft the trembling maid.

As the keen failor, whom his daring foul

Has drawn, too vent'rous, near the freezing pole ;

Who, having flighted caution's tame advice,

Seems wedg'd within impervious worlds of ice ;

If, from each chilling form of peril free,

At length he reach the unincumber'd fea,

With joy fuperior to his tranfient pain,

Rufhes, exulting, o'er th' expanfive main :

Such ftrong delight SERENA's bofom fhar'd,

When fweet reflection to her heart declar'd,

That

That all the trials of her fate were paſt,

. And love's deciſive plaudit ſeal'd the laſt.

Her airy guard prepares the ſofteſt down,

From peace's wing, to line the nuptial crown :

Her ſmiles accelerate the bridal morn,

And clear her votary's path from every thorn.

On the quick match the prude's keen cenſures fall,

Blind to the heavenly power who guided all :

. But mild SERENA ſcorn'd the prudiſh play,

To wound warm love with frivolous delay ;

Nature's chaſte child, not affeſtation's ſlave,

The heart ſhe meant to give, ſhe frankly gave.

Thro' her glad ſire no gouty humours run,

Jocund he glories in his deſtin'd ſon.

PENELOPE herſelf, no longer ſeen

.. In the four ſemblance of tormenting Spleen,

Buys for her niece the robes of nuptial ſtate,

Nor ſcolds the mercer once thro' all the long debate.

For quick diſpatch, the honeſt man of law

Toils half the night the legal ties to draw ;

At

At length th' enraptur'd youth, all forms compleat,
Bears his fweet bride to his paternal feat;
On a fair lawn the chearful manfion ftood,
And high behind it rofe a circling wood.
As the bleft lord of this extenfive reign
Led his dear partner thro' her new domain,
With fond furprife, SERENA foon defcried
A temple rais'd to her ætherial guide.
Its ornaments fhe view'd with tender awe,
Their fafhion fuch as fhe in vifion faw;
For the kind youth, her grateful fmile to gain,
Had, from her clear defcription, deck'd the fane.
Joyful he cried, to his angelic wife,
" Be this kind power the worfhip of our life!"
He fpoke; and led her to the inmoft fhrine;
Here, link'd in rofy bands, two votaries fhine;
The pencil had imparted life to each,
With energy that feem'd beyond its reach.
Firft ftood Connubial Love, a manly youth,
Whofe bright eye fpoke the ardent vows of truth;

M   Friendfhip,

Friendſhip, ſweet ſmiling, fill'd the ſecond place,

In all the ſofter charms of virgin grace.

Their meeting arms a myſtic tablet raiſe,

Deck'd with theſe lines, the moral of my lays :—

"VIRTUE's an ingot of Peruvian gold,

SENSE the bright ore Potoſi's mines unfold ;

But TEMPER's image muſt their uſe create,

And give theſe precious metals ſterling weight."

F I N I S.